THE RELUCTANT BARONET

THE RELUCTANT BARONET

Jane Gillespie

Chivers Press • Thorndike Press
Bath, England Thorndike, Maine USA

This Large Print edition is published by Chivers Press, England, and by Thorndike Press, USA.

Published in 1999 in the U.K. by arrangement with Robert Hale Ltd.

Published in 1999 in the U.S. by arrangement with Robert Hale Limited.

U.K. Hardcover ISBN 0–7540–3595–6 (Chivers Large Print)
U.K. Softcover   ISBN 0–7540–3596–4 (Camden Large Print)
U.S. Softcover   ISBN 0–7862–1701–4 (General Series Edition)

The text of this Large Print edition is unabridged.
Other aspects of the book may vary from the original edition.

Set in 16 pt. New Times Roman.

Printed in Great Britain on acid-free paper.

British Library Cataloguing in Publication Data available

Library of Congress Cataloging-in-Publication Data

Gillespie, Jane, 1923–
        The reluctant baronet / Jane Gillespie.
            p.   cm.
        ISBN 0–7862–1701–4 (lg. print : sc : alk. paper)
        1. Large type books.   I. Title.
        [PR6057.I574R4   1999]
        823'.914—dc21
                                                                98–44508

CHAPTER ONE

A gentleman not yet forty years of age who inherits a baronetcy, a large estate in the English Midlands and several plantations in the West Indies and is, moreover, still a bachelor, may expect life to hold many pleasures in store for him.

The gentleman in question viewed his future with some misgiving. He had devoted his youth to his own pleasures but had as the years passed grown more steady, and willingly joined with his father the baronet in the administration of his properties, finding the task not uninteresting. It was only as grief for his father gave way to a more practical appreciation of his father's absence, that a wind of change blew upon him with an unwelcome chill. It began to appear that, in future, decisions would devolve upon the new baronet and responsibility would be his. Responsibility was what he had always avoided. Perhaps this was why he had not taken upon himself the obligations of a husband. He had spent much of his time on the family estate in Northamptonshire because of his many sporting interests, but kept a house in London because he had many interests in town too. After his father's funeral he had so many delays, with lawyers and stewards, that he

1

almost despaired of resuming his town life; when he did return to London he was full of discouragement and gloom, and promptly visited his sister in Marylebone to tell her so.

Mrs Yates was not unsympathetic. 'Indeed I was afraid this sad inheritance would bring some new troubles upon you—'

'It is nothing but troubles, according to those tedious old lawmen. I knew that my father was constantly worried about money and spoke as if the estate were on the verge of ruin—but we lived well enough. He spent nothing on himself—even, he gave up the town house and he watched over the household expenses as if we were on the edge of poverty—I am sure none of my friends were kept so short you know—'

His sister remarked in gentle reproof: 'He laid out a large amount of money in the settlement of your gaming debts at one time, if you remember—'

'*Pah*—A young man's frivolities! I knew a dozen friends who played higher. Nor did I repeat my offences.—And now it seems that the whole estate *is* in peril. Why? I do not understand. Why, for instance, did he not sell off those plantations in Jamaica, which are nothing but an encumbrance?'

'Perhaps because he could not find a buyer. The anti-slavery movement is growing stronger—'

'*Pah*. How could one make a profit of such

an enterprise without cheap labour?'

'That must have been our father's predicament.'

From loyalty, the new baronet did not complain that his father had bequeathed the predicament to him. He muttered: 'Well, I do not know what is to be done. And I will tell you another thing that amazes me: These good mercenary hacks assure me that the whole estate is actually on the point of collapse and they had the impudence to suggest that we *let* it.'

'Let it? Let Mansfield? To strangers?' This alarmed her.

'I told them of course that that could not be considered.'

'Certainly it could not—where could you stable your horses, to start with? And what would our mother do?'

They both fell reflectively silent, till Mrs Yates murmured: 'I feel that leaving Mansfield would break her heart, if it were not already broken. How was she when you left her?'

'... The same, quiet and tearful, but sitting there with her embroidery and pugs ...' He half shrugged and his sister nodded. Their mother was a serene and easy-going person, indulged by her husband and all about her, occupied by needlework, unmoved by the tumults of the world: how she would be affected by her widowhood her children could not yet conjecture. She was not without

3

feelings, but in her tranquil existence she rarely had the need of expressing them. Hitherto, her husband had been able to tell her what she felt; at present, it was as if she awaited his advice still; she wept and embroidered and might descend into apathy. Her daughter, frowning, now said:

'I wish I might have stayed longer with her after the obsequies. But John had to be back in town. I might go to visit her alone for a while, to bear her company. She should not be lonely. I suppose she has Susan.'

'Well, but she always has Susan. I shall have to go down there myself again in a week or two. But I cannot *stay*—though they seem to think it my duty.' He sighed heavily.

Mrs Yates pursuing her own thoughts said: 'Do you know, I should not at all mind being at Mansfield for a while. The spring is coming on, and I had forgotten how pleasant that can be in the country. Were we not happy there as children, Tom? Yet as soon as I was older I found the country so dull and I could not wait to get away from it and into town—'

'And so you did. I do not know what you find to complain of. Here you have your town life and friends and enough money and no one lays burdens on you or drives you hither and thither—'

'I am not complaining,' Mrs Yates denied, still pensive. 'In truth I am recollecting my good fortune, and am fully aware of it.'

She had reason to be. In the young womanhood that succeeded her happy country childhood, she had made a runaway marriage with the Honourable John Yates, whom she had known for a scarce few weeks. A crisis in the family, threatening disgrace and scandal, made her snatch at any means of escape, and her good fortune consisted in the happiness of her marriage. Her John, as she made his acquaintance, proved to be generous, amusing, and kind; they had many interests in common, a wide social circle in London, and two delightful children. It was understandable that she did not willingly visit, or even look back on, Mansfield Park and the quarrels and jealousies of her girlhood. As she now looked back she recognized how peaceful these recent years had been; everyone had been contented: Tom agreeable and helpful to his father in estate matters, her younger brother, in orders, happy in the Mansfield parsonage with his demure little wife, and her elder sister (source of all the disruption and scandal) living abroad. Inevitably, the death of Sir Thomas would bring about changes, but she hoped that the new Sir Thomas would not be made difficult and restless. He was a friend of her husband John, and they had shared interests in town, important to John. He and Tom had become owners of a theatre off The Strand and John was ambitious to secure a larger place and to stage larger productions. It had been suggested that Tom should be half-owner of this too; but if he were to spend more of his time at Mansfield and to have less money at his disposal, what would become of that project? Mrs Yates dared not broach the topic today, while Tom was so disgruntled.

In any case, he was leaving; he had to visit a *solicitor* (he spoke the word with disgust) in 'Holborn or somewhere . . .' His sister went to the window to watch him tramping off down the street, glum and slouching under the mourning band of his hat, not looking a very fine figure of a baronet.

CHAPTER TWO

Spring had come to Mansfield Park, and the gardens and woods were bright with blossom and birdsong. Indoors, however, mourning still reigned. Mirrors were veiled, voices even in the kitchens were hushed. Lady Bertram worked at her embroidery, but with frequent pauses: the tears on her cheeks fell, unheeded. She closed her eyes as if falling asleep although little sighs escaped her. She did not like to be idle, though to many people her life might not have seemed perceptibly active at the best of times. And at this time, surely the worst, bereft of her husband's care and comfort, it was no small wonder that she was lost.

The door of the room opened and closed as someone quietly entered. Without opening her eyes Lady Bertram said: 'Susan, my head is aching a little. Where is my vinaigrette?' She knew that it was Susan; Susan was never far away; less than ever, since the loss of Sir Thomas could Lady Bertram have done without Susan at all.

Susan Price, a niece of Lady Bertram, was willing to be both indispensable and solicitous. She had lived at Mansfield Park for many years now, after arriving ostensiby on a visit when she was fourteen years old, in the wake of that family crisis that was now fading from history, but that had made her fresh and helpful presence welcome.

She had grown into the household willingly; she had just reached her thirtieth birthday, remaining grateful and attentive; she was sympathetic but practical. Now she provided the vinaigrette, and from a cabinet added a small glass of cordial; picking up a skein of silk that had fallen to the floor she seated herself beside her aunt, saying:

'I have written to Lady Morwell, ma'am, and I will send the letter about the Oak Farm tenancy to Tom in London.'

Lady Bertram sighed more deeply. 'Tom should be here to help me in all these matters,' she said. 'They are too much for me to deal with or to understand.'

7

It can be believed that Lady Bertram had made no attempt to deal with the condolences that were still being received, or to turn her mind to business affairs; also that as she sat idle, Susan had been fully occupied with them.

'Tom will be coming soon,' Susan assured her, adding: 'He promised,' to assure herself; more confidently she went on: 'And tomorrow, you remember, Julia is coming to visit you.'

'Is she to bring her children?'

'Just Decima, Mortimer is at school.'

'I do not know that I want people visiting. I do not feel equal to company.'

'I expect Decima will spend her time at the Parsonage with her cousins, you know. Julia feels she needs country air—Decima, I mean. And none of the Yates family has been often at Mansfield—'

'Then why should they come now, when I am so distracted?'

'They may not stay for very long.'

'No, I suppose it will be dull for them here,' said Lady Bertram between relief and pique. She turned her attention to her work and took a stitch. 'This white thread is too strong. I cannot manage it.'

'There is some finer in your basket; I shall find it . . .' But Lady Bertram had lost interest; her needle flagged and she closed her eyes. Susan watched her expecting tears. But after a while Lady Bertram said in a musing tone:

'I was thinking, you know. If I go into half

8

mourning, it will by then be—October? And I could have a grey gown—two grey gowns—made up from the material that Madame Louise was showing me in the winter. Perhaps with a trimming of white lace. And a sash of black velvet . . . Or purple . . .'

Susan bent her head lest her aunt should observe the smile that this surprised from her. 'That would be very . . . suitable,' she said, gravely. She dare not suggest that her aunt sought elegance or would look handsome in her half-mourning; but indeed, Lady Bertram for all her sixty years was still a pretty woman; even the ravages of grief had not marred her complexion, smooth as it was after the years of untroubled life. It was encouraging to discover that she could look ahead, for even a half year. Susan pursued:

'And for going out of doors, we might make veils for some of your bonnets—perhaps from the lace that we used for your widow's caps—' in which, too, Lady Bertram looked appealing. She did not however accept this idea at all.

'Oh no. I shall not need bonnets, because I shall not be going out. Not for the full year. If ever. I do not care for visiting, as you well know. I shall be content to stay at home in my own dear rooms and remember the happy times of the past.' This brought tears again. Susan uttering no unavailing words of consolation took up the sewing basket and hunted for the finer white thread.

She felt that a point had been made, and some progress achieved. It was impossible to mention the scheme for the letting of the house of which Tom had told her. It was impossible to imagine a change like that for Lady Bertram. Tom must be dissuaded, and if perchance he had seen Julia in town and mentioned it to her, Susan must dissuade Julia too. She was only a niece—one might say, a poor relation in the family, but she was as concerned for her aunt as anyone. Lady Bertram had shown that she might take up her life again on her own terms, and surely that must be permitted to her. Susan had not devoted so many years to serving her aunt without establishing an unshakeable affection for her, and a determination to defend her, if need be, against the rest of her family. And Susan herself had more determination than the family might suppose.

CHAPTER THREE

When Julia and Decima arrived on the following day, Lady Bertram was in plaintive mood and soon tired of the company. Decima, a lively girl with a good deal to say for herself, observed that she was not holding her grandmother's attention and became restless; Julia announced: 'I think we have had enough of your chatter, my dear,' and bade her go to visit the Parsonage. Decima sped off down the park, released, and Lady Bertram slipped into a doze.

It was of her daughter that Julia first spoke as she and Susan stepped out to stroll on the terrace, Julia feeling the need of air after the fatigue of travel. 'It is country air that I am sure Decima needs,' she said. 'Her complexion is not good and she should take more exercise. She is sixteen now, you know, and will be "out" very soon. Since her governess left, she is frittering her time in town and also choosing unsuitable company. She wants to be an actress, naturally.'

It may not have seemed natural that a young girl in Decima's position should aspire to a career on the stage, but Susan knew—and a touch of irony in Julia's tone reminded her—that the theatre had played a large part in the life of the Yates family. The Honourable John, enthralled in his youth by amateur theatricals, had as he grew older come to take the stage more seriously; no actor himself, he gave his attention to production, studying all types of drama, and presenting verse drama, Shakepeare, and opera; fortunately his private fortune enabled him to support the financial loss on some of his more ambitious ventures, of which the acquisition of his own theatre was the most recent, and in which he hoped to be joined by his old friend Tom Bertram—or Sir

Thomas, should he now say? Tom was as fascinated by theatrical matters as John Yates, and gave them as much attention and money as he could spare from his horse-racing and gaming.

Susan remarked to Julia, as they turned at the end of the terrace:

'I can see Decima as a clever and pretty little actress.'

'So can she,' said Decima's mother. 'But apart from that, I cannot allow her to associate with professional theatre folk. They are a raffish lot, with neither scruples nor morals. It was unwise to let the governess go, and I am the more glad now to have Decima away from town awhile.'

'She will come under no such infuence as you mention, at the Parsonage,' said Susan smiling. 'Though she will find it hard not to chatter to her grandmother. This house will be too quiet for her.'

Julia paused to sit on the balustrade as Susan went indoors to see how Lady Bertram did. When Susan returned to report that Lady Bertram was still asleep, Julia sighed.

'In my opinion it is too quiet here altogether just now.' The sun was going down; long shadows crossed the empty acres of parkland and only a distant cawing of rooks was heard. 'Tell me, do you find any improvement yet in my mother? I had hoped to. I feel, though, that she is more withdrawn than she was a few weeks ago. She is making no effort . . .' Her voice faded, as both she and Susan wondered whether Lady Bertram had ever made anything so vigorous as an effort over anything. Susan took up:

'No, but it may come to her naturally in time, to take up her life again. Only yesterday . . .' and she described her aunt's unexpected raising of the matter of half-mourning. 'She was for a while quite animated.'

Julia listened with a frown. 'I suppose that she will wear mourning dress for the rest of her life. Clothes are not important—'

'To her, they are,' Susan countered. 'In so far as anything is. We should not expect too much.'

'But on the other hand we should stimulate her. Do you know, I begin to change my mind about her leaving Mansfield—'

'Tom told you about that? About letting the place?'

'Yes, and at first I felt we could not possibly do so—That it would be too grievous for her altogether. But I am afraid that it might prove to be necessary. Tom will have difficulties—more I think than he yet suspects. It was my father who saw to the financial affairs of the estates and kept them within bounds. Tom—though I am his sister, I must admit it—is extravagant by nature. He keeps up his house in town, and his racing stables, and has committed himself recklessly to our theatrical

13

plans—Mr Yates is indeed anxious on his account. I tell this to you in confidence; but you know Tom and might understand.'

Susan did understand; she knew from Tom, and moreover knew all Julia had divulged, but she did not say so. She nodded solemnly.

'So you see,' Julia resumed, 'that for his own sake we must take any course that preserves the family's solvency. If that means letting the Park and finding a fresh home for my mother, we must make it a happy change. Surely that is possible. She is easily contented in herself, and some distraction would help her to take up her life again.' Julia's tone took on the briskness of self-persuasion. 'She likes the country, but she would be the better for a little social life. In Bath, for instance, we might find a quiet house where she could make a few friends in similar circumstances to hers, and take there her favourite furnishings from here, and her dogs. You would go with her, of course.'

Julia was well disposed towards Susan and meant this kindly; it was not that she considered Susan to be of secondary importance to the dogs, or removable as an item of furniture. Rather she felt she was generous, in offering Susan a new home; because what otherwise would become of her?

Julia had seen little of Susan, and considered her less; she valued Susan as her mother's companion, perhaps the more as she herself had not been a very attentive daughter.

14

Of Susan herself, apart from Susan as Lady Bertram's invaluable companion, Julia was heedless; Susan was always calm, practical, unobtrusive; evidently she was satisfied with her life and status at Mansfield; and this was as well, because for all her looks—tall and slender, with a fine complexion and large dark eyes—she could not expect to marry. If she now said nothing to Julia's offer of her removal to Bath, that was only what Julia expected and required. They turned again at the end of the terrace and as Julia said: 'Well, let us go indoors—' they did so, Susan's dark eyes lowered. They had had, Julia felt, a useful conference.

Susan was fully aware that Julia would welcome no opinion of hers, and was not offended. In general, she had been used to giving her opinions to Sir Thomas and Lady Bertram and to Tom, when asked, which frequently occurred; Sir Thomas had confided in her his business worries and valued her clear mind; Lady Bertram asked what Susan thought, on every particular, before making any small decision; Tom asked what he was supposed to *do* in any frustration, then laughed at her advice and forgot it. In her apparently quiet way Susan had gained over the years a position of some authority in the household.

When first she came to Mansfield Park she was awed by the size and splendour of the house and by the dignified manners of the

15

family, in contrast to the noise and uncouthness of the home she had left. This phase did not last for long. Not only had she the guidance and support of her elder sister who had been rescued similarly by the Bertrams some while ago, but she had a spirit of independence and courage that enabled her to take her own decisions and to abide by them privately. A decision she took shortly after settling at Mansfield was of a surprising precocity but of a firmness that still obtained and had had its own part perhaps in forming her character.

She succeeded to the place of adviser and help to Lady Bertram when her elder sister married, moving only across the park to be the wife of the younger Bertram son, clergyman of the parish. At this development Susan reached her decision. She was fond of Lady Bertram already and grateful for all the kindness she had known here, but with Sir Thomas's gravity and Lady Bertram's vagueness, she irresistibly felt most at ease with Cousin Tom, who teased her and made her laugh and brought her favours from fairs and a kitten from among the straw bales of the stables. 'But,' decided Susan, 'I shall not fall in love with him.'

This was indeed a rash decision to make at the age of fourteen, before she knew anything of the tender passions, or attributed any great importance to them, but possibly Susan's reasoning was the clearer for that. She knew that it was not considered wise for cousins to marry; it had happened between two of these already but surely Sir Thomas would not approve of a second such alliance. She knew that Tom was to be a baronet and should have a wife to grace the rank, which Susan, poorly educated, socially inept, not beautiful (such was her opinion of herself at fourteen and it was not altogether unfounded) could not aspire to. And she had understood already, from conversations overheard between Tom and his father, that the Bertrams, in spite of the splendour of their possessions to Susan's eyes, were not as wealthy as it appeared, and that should Tom acquire a wife of even moderate fortune, that would be highly acceptable.

Susan found all this reasonable, as in fact it was. At fourteen she was a reasonable being, and content with her conclusions. As the years passed and Tom produced no wife of any kind, Tom continued to tease Susan and complain to her of his troubles—but then, so he treated everyone—and Susan too treated him as she treated everyone. Supposing a lady can decide not to fall in love, she had done so. When Sir Thomas, who found her so helpful in business matters, told her: 'I believe that you know more about the running of the place than Tom does, my dear!' she gave a deprecating smile with no comment. She was always neat and cool and pleasant; no one knew what she was thinking; no one, in view of her composure, wondered.

CHAPTER FOUR

Julia returned to town dissatisfied; nothing had been achieved during the weeks at Mansfield; many matters were still to be settled before the scheme of letting the Park, and its effect on Lady Bertram, could be broached; too many of Julia's own affairs had gathered for her attention; and, worse, the spring greenery of Northamptonshire had already been succeeded by the dust and heat of London summer. Worst, perhaps: Decima had gained nothing from country air but freckles and an increasingly hoydenish manner after the constraint of the mourning house and the decorous Parsonage. She whirled into the drawingroom where her mother was writing letters and her father brooding over his newspaper, to proclaim:

'Mama, Caroline has called for me and we are going to look at some new muslins at a shop in Welbeck Street—'

'You cannot want to walk about the town in this heat,' said Julia, trying to catch a sheet of writing paper that her daughter's entry had blown off her table, while it brought a gritty draught from the open window. Decima pouncing for the paper insisted:

'But they are beautiful and quite new. Barbara was telling me.'

'Who pray is Barbara?'

'Oh—you know. She sings. I must go—Caroline is waiting—'

John Yates looked up from his newspaper. 'Miss Blake, did you mention? Is she here now? I was hoping to have a word with her.'

'Oh but we want to go shopping—'

'Muslins can wait,' declared Julia, 'and so can you. Please ask Miss Blake to come up, and then have your hair dressed. It looks like a hayfield. Then we will see about shopping, perhaps.'

Pouting, Decima flounced out of the room. John Yates folding his newspaper remarked: 'I cannot imagine that Miss Blake is in eager pursuit of beautiful muslins.'

'Nor I. I wish she were. She is much too serious.'

'And intent on her own eager pursuit. I wish we could help her. I feel partly responsible—'

'Well, but you are not. You are too soft-hearted at times,' Julia told him without reproach. 'Let us see what she says to my latest suggestion. She is so proud—in her way . . .' She broke off as the door quietly opened and Decima's friend, unannounced and hesitant, entered the room.

It would have been obvious at first glance that the young woman curtseying to Julia was

19

not one of the undesirable friends whom Julia feared Decima to have acquired from her new theatrical circles. Caroline was slight, delicately formed, modest in her bearing and soberly dressed. Her hesitancy came from polite deference rather than from shyness, though a second glance would reveal that her simple clothes were carefully mended and her hair however tidy was styled by no *coiffeuse*. She had fine enough features but the pallor of her cheeks was emphasised by the blue hollows under her eyes. Her whole appearance spoke of poverty, anxiety and a natural dignity. John Yates, greeting her with: 'Good day to you— Are you quite well, m-Miss Blake...?' checked himself from the 'my dear...' which would have offended against her formality. She thanked him and assured him that she was quite well, a statement that a glance exchanged between Julia and her husband agreed in disbelieving. Miss Blake was under-nourished, tired, and suffering like everyone from the lassitude of dusty London. Julia thought: The more sorry I am for her, the less I feel I should say so. In ways she is wrong-headed but one has to respect her.

In setting forth today to Miss Blake a project that should be to her advantage, even Julia felt a tremor of awkwardness. It was true though that as soon as they knew her story both Julia and John had felt an unhappy sympathy for her.

Caroline Blake came from the north country, where her father was clergyman of a parish in the wilds of Westmorland. He had died when Caroline and her brother were small children, and his widow had returned to the home of her father, a just but stern gentleman who owned a sheep-farming estate on the further and even wilder Pennines. Here the children were tolerated and enjoyed their games and ploys together about the moorland; the unwritten rule was merely that they keep out of Grandfather's way. No strife arose until the matter of Stephen's education began to occupy their mother. After the village school, what was to be done with him? He was more than clever; he was brilliant. Indeed he had genius. He was a poet, a rare spirit. His mother was convinced of this and so was Caroline. His grandfather admitted that the boy had brains, but as for poetry—Nonsense. He must buckle down and find work that would enable him to support his mother and sister. Well then, Mr Holroyd his grandfather finally conceded, he might go to Sedbergh, or some school like that, and turn into a clergyman like his father, and to university if he needed Latin for any reason, and for this his grandfather would pay—But this would be in the form of a loan, let Stephen mark this—a loan that he would repay when he was trained and earning.

So Stephen received his education, and Caroline and his mother stitched at his shirts and sent him parcels of cake and apples, and all three of them lived in the faith of his future—not in some academic drudgery or commercial labour, but in freedom, his spirit revealing the pure glory that exceeds any gain of money. Such hopes were not confided in Mr Holroyd, but at one point Mrs Blake urged Caroline:

'When he leaves Cambridge, you know, he must not come back here. It is too remote; I am sure he should go to London, where he may meet people, face to face—It is no use, writing letters and sending copies of poems when one is quite unknown ...' For already various selections of poems had been sent to various publishers and received with no gratitude.

'I wish you and I might go with him,' sighed Caroline, who had her own reasons for wishing to leave her grandfather's domain. He had told her several times that it was time she married, and had introduced to her the son of a prosperous wool merchant who had a shooting box nearby. He was a pleasant young man but Caroline's affections were set only on Stephen and his muse.

'I wish we might,' sighed Mrs Blake, spreading her hands in a gesture that illustrated: But what should we live on?

This consideration, as it turned out, was disregarded after an unforeseen and tragic turn of events during Stephen's last term at

22

Cambridge: Mrs Blake, never robust, died after a short illness. She was conscious to the last, and her last whisper to Caroline who held her hand was: 'Stephen . . .' in a faint plea that Caroline fully understood. 'Yes, Mama, I will do my best for him,' she promised, which earned her her mother's last smile.

Stephen could not arrive from Cambridge before his mother died and he found the funeral unutterably distressing. It threw him into a despair equal to Caroline's; neither could have said which of them first spoke the desperate words: Let us go to London!

So they fled, overnight, casting themselves as it were into the current of fate. Stephen would not return to Cambridge; he cared nothing for his degree. Caroline in spite of her grief was glad to make this negative defiance of her grandfather; it gave her courage. And indeed Stephen, released, was surprised by the vigour of his poetic energy, and became absorbed by the writing of a verse drama on the death of Socrates, which had been taking shape in the back of his mind. They found lodgings in the house of an elderly aunt of a Cambridge friend of his; Caroline sold some of her mother's scanty pieces of jewellery; the relief of their escape gave them a wondering happiness; could they at last be free—Too free? Stephen, abandoned to his creative frenzy, became reckless himself. He wrote day and night, with little time to eat, and no time to visit publishers, which would have afforded him some respite. Inspiration lagging, he would wander out along the river in its dawn vapours until Caroline came to search for him; he would protest: 'No, no, I am quite happy— Just thinking—But, my dear, you must not come out in the cold like this!'

It was their elderly landlady who said: 'That brother of yours is not at all well, miss. You need him to have the apothecary.'

But their money was almost gone. Caroline had been working for a local seamstress, pretending not to be hungry, undressing in the dark to save candles, doing all she could to protect Stephen; but even so, she knew she could not save him; he lived only in his work; and even now, he would rather finish his verse drama than live. And so he finished it; and so he died.

And so he was buried a pauper, in a strange city; and so Caroline was alone in a strange city, a living pauper, twenty six years old, with no friends or family. She had of course notified her grandfather of Stephen's death, and received in return a curt command that she must return to his house. As she had given this address, she changed it as soon as possible, and thought herself fortunate to find a lady offering an attic room free to someone who would sit up at nights to tend an aged grandmother. By day, after a short sleep, Caroline set about the one sustaining purpose of her life: To keep faith with her mother and Stephen by achieving the publication of his work.

While Stephen was with her she had known that she could not help him in this; she could not approach strange publishers or plead his cause. Now, strangely enough, she found it entirely possible. At night, if the aged grandmother slept, Caroline could settle by a shaded candle to copying poems and drama; by day she could carry on the work for the seamstress; she was fully occupied. It was at about this time that she met Decima Yates, during an exploration of the streets beyond Drury Lane. Caroline was grown bold now and would walk long distances, and inquire of any person, in her quest. She saw across the street a theatre of fair size and stylish design, bearing the name 'Orion'. Its doors were open to the morning air and a boy in an apron was sweeping the steps, meanwhile exchanging chat with two young girls within. Caroline approached inquiring:

'If you please—who is the owner of this theatre?'

The boy's broom paused as he gaped at her, but one of the girls took it upon herself to answer. She danced down the steps saying:

'I do not know, but my father intends to be.'

'So at the moment the theatre is not in commission?'

'Nothing is being staged here, no. Are you

an actress?'

The notion struck Caroline as absurd and she smiled a little. 'I am asking on behalf of a dramatist who is anxious to stage his play,' she explained. She could not use the past tense in speaking of Stephen.

'Well I hope your dramatist is not in a great hurry,' returned the girl, 'since my father is having difficulty in raising the money.' She glanced again at Caroline, whose disappointment must have shown on her face, for she added seriously: 'Perhaps my father may know of a theatre for you. He knows a great many people with theatres. I will ask him, if you want me to.'

Any gleam of hope Caroline dared not refuse. She said: 'It might be more fitting were I to ask him myself. Would you tell me his name and where I might approach him?'

'Yes, I will give you our address—Barbara, have you a sheet of paper and a pencil?' Barbara had, and she provided them with some impatience, muttering: 'Come *along*, Dessie—I am supposed to be at my music lesson—' and the pair of them ran off, leaving Caroline with the address of Mr Yates, to whom she wrote one of her usual polite—and, she felt, unpersuasive—letters. She did not suppose the girl would remember her, or if so, describe her to her father except as a shabby eccentric.

She misjudged Decima, who had formed a

pleasing estimate of her and whose curiosity was aroused by someone who went about looking for a theatre; she told Mr Yates: 'She was obviously a *lady*, Papa, and she looked so dowdy and sad. If she does write to you, you will reply, I hope?'

In the first instance her father was only indignant that Decima should prattle about his financial affairs all about town and to strangers.

'But, Papa, everyone knows that you want to buy the Orion—'

'Do not answer me back in that pert fashion, miss. As for calling the woman a lady—I wish I thought anyone could say the same of you.' Decima was mortified into silence, and afraid that her father would ignore any letter that the sad lady wrote.

The Honourable John, annoyed by his daughter's indiscretion, would have had to admit that it must be widely known that the sale of the Orion was held up. He may have been by most standards wealthy, but he was not unwise. The man who survives is the spend-thrift who knows when to stop spending; lately he had suffered some embarrassment over his investments and chose to be cautious. He wanted—almost coveted—that theatre but another impediment had arisen: his dear friend Tom Bertram had promised a large part of the price but now apparently that was not forthcoming. When the two of them sold their poky little theatre in Warwick Street, Tom had pocketed his share of the proceeds willingly and John had supposed that, after his father's death, Tom would have more money at his disposal; but, quite to the contrary, Tom was grousing away as if he had been rendered destitute and the dear old friendship was in some peril. John Yates was restless, needing something to occupy his attention and he was, in fact, not scornful of the mildly expressed letter that he duly received from this Caroline Blake—wife of the Stephen Blake mentioned as the author?—and he did reply, agreeing to read the manuscript but stating firmly that he had no way of staging the play. When the play, neatly packaged, and most neatly penned throughout, was delivered by carrier he read it and not without interest. His own tastes had matured since his youth and he had grown impatient with the melodramas and sentimental romances that his theatre manager insisted that audiences insisted on. This manuscript displayed the quality fitting the Orion theatre as John envisaged it; the title— 'The Death of Wisdom'—was perhaps a little forbidding; why not, for instance, 'The Triumph of Wisdom'? He threw down the pages, checking his ever too ready enthusiasm. He must meet this Stephen Blake and deny him, to the frustration of them both. Verse dramas and unknown poets thronged the city. And when he heard of the demise of Stephen

Blake he was further discouraged. The work of an unknown poet was a risk, but were it also posthumous it was doubly handicapped.

He did not enjoy explaining this to the poet's sister, but he found that she was not cast down. Her purpose could apparently withstand discouragement; John was impressed by her manner and promised to inquire among his theatrical acquaintances and do what he could for her cause, which was all he could say. Since his daughter Decima held herself responsible for the introduction, and since she seemed to have formed an admiration for Miss Blake and wished to make a friend of her, Miss Blake was invited to drink tea with the family. She told little of herself and no one pressed her; Julia noticed that Decima when in Miss Blake's presence behaved in a fashion that could fairly be called 'ladylike'; this item of interest may have lingered in the mother's mind during the long visit to Mansfield Park, because when she returned to London still dissatisfied with her daughter's conduct, her mind turned to Miss Blake as a possible remedy. This was what she had decided to mention on this dusty afternoon while Decima was finding a bonnet in which to go shopping for muslins.

'Decima would not tolerate another governess but she is in need of a little guidance and good example. It would be only for a few months, until she is "out"; we could lodge you in the house and leave you free for much of the time; it is just that we would be glad to know, when she runs about the town, where she is and with whom.'

'For instance,' put in Decima's father, in a grumpy tone, 'what were she and that other girl doing at the Orion, when you first encountered her? The theatre is no concern of hers. Yet.'

Caroline's face had seemed to grow cold and stiff. Julia after hesitating, anticipating a refusal, risked adding: 'We would give you a small fee, of course—just pin-money.'

This provoked neither refusal nor gratitude. Caroline was deep in calculation. For some time now she had been hard at work, trying to save up enough money to pay for the printing of Stephen's poems. One of the publishers who rejected them had suggested it; she had not known it possible, nor did she imagine she could amass such an amount, but determination had kept her by the hour stitching—in the fine stitching her mother had taught her, that they had employed on shirts for Stephen—until her head throbbed and her eyesight failed. Today she saw everything through spangling dark stars and knew she must break off. She had been glad to keep her promise to Decima but afraid the effort in such heat would provide little relief. And now, this offer of Mrs Yates' took her by surprise and she forced herself to think. Decima, she felt, was grown fond of her but Caroline could not

30

allow herself to become fond of anyone. At closer quarters, how demanding would Decima prove? She was not a creature to be repressed. The family was not one to be civilly turned aside. Mr Yates had been kinder to Caroline than any of the theatrical people she had approached, and still had her interests in mind, she knew. What was 'pin-money'? Scruples would never let Caroline accept an unearned recompense. Living in this house, could she wear the scanty much-mended clothes—all she had? Especially if she were going about the town with Decima; to what Caroline wore, she herself was by now indifferent. There was however one circumstance that had an undeniable importance: She was perhaps on the point of losing her present lodging: the grandmother of Mrs Esher, Caroline's charge during the night hours, was beginning to fail quickly; Mrs Esher had more than once remarked to Caroline that she must soon employ professional nurses.

So Caroline brought her few possessions to the house of the Yateses, where she made little stir and roused little interest, so unobtrusive was she, and so little concerned with her surroundings. As it was, there was always coming and going: shiftless hangers-on seeking the attention of John Yates, fringes of theatrical life ready for a free meal in the servants' hall, where Caroline joined them and they probably took her for a failed actress or extra seamstress; Decima who did indeed admire Caroline was tactful in requests for Caroline's company and happy in it. The 'pin-money' was handed over in an envelope once a week by the housekeeper, and the fund in Caroline's purse, an old leather one of Stephen's, began very slowly to increase.

CHAPTER FIVE

At about this time a friend of the Yateses', who had a large house in a nearby square and a good deal of money, was planning to stage in his ballroom an amateur production of what he called a 'musical drama' with the title of 'Ondine', adapted from the legend by a composer of his acquaintance, and having as its showpiece one professional soprano, the eminent German Hilde Buchspiel. Decima had hoped that the producer, Mr Stein—and her parents—might offer her a part, but, overlooked, she took a great interest in the affair, and one afternoon persuaded Caroline to walk with her and see whether a rehearsal was under way.

As it happened there was not, but there was much activity over some difficult stage effects. The stage hands, Mr Stein's household servants, were enjoying this novelty in their regular duties and the occasion was waxing hilarious. It appeared that a large stone blocking the well in the castle courtyard had to be lifted, and a fountain to emerge, and turn into the figure of Ondine, who then moved sadly off to the destruction of her faithless knight. This was effective on the page, but quite how it was to be performed on the stage was giving more trouble. There was a platform at the end of the room under which Ondine could be concealed, and there would be great swaths of white lace to represent the water of the fountain, but how to bring Ondine gracefully forth? They practised on the smallest servant—a boot boy—who shot up like a jack-in-the-box, tripped over the edge of the slanting stone and fell flat on his face. Besides, how was Ondine to extricate herself from the lace without tangling herself in that? Decima cried: 'Oh please try it on me. I am sure I am no heavier than this boy—'

'Nay, miss, you're a fair armful and we can't have you falling—'

'We'll need to be down the well ourselves to hoist her up. That'll look silly to start with.'

'Two of us could be below, maybe, and two others shift the stone, and stay under—'

'Easy to make the stone look heavy, but we can't have a lumping great water-nymph or whatever they call her. Come on Stanley, get down your well again, lad.'

'I do wish I—' began Decima, but Caroline put a restraining hand on her shoulder, presuming that her duties as chaperone to Decima would not include allowing her to be thrown about by boisterous manservants.

'Wait.'

This command silenced the gathering; Mr Stein had arrived, after having his wife find a length of lace suitable to the fountain. He advanced shaking out the lace, saying:

'Let us have some order about this. It seems to me that this other lady is lighter even than Stanley and holds herself straight. Will you try it without the lace first, ma'am?'

'Oh *yes*. Caroline!' exclaimed Decima. Caroline, with her air of indifferent obedience, submitted herself to be helped into the well; she recognized in Mr Stein the single-mindedness that must have the thing just right; she told the men beside her: 'If you give me a count of three and then take me firmly round the waist—' As they obeyed her she threw up her arms and balanced on the edge of the well, calling: '—And place my right foot *here*— thank you. Supposing you two,' she added to the stone-movers, 'were to jump up and look astonished, it might hide my movements in case they are clumsy.'

Astonished they were, and Mr Stein hurrying forward with his lace cried: 'Yes, yes—That was the effect I wanted—' He had no idea who this 'other lady' was but he must have her as Ondine—who was in any case a non-speaking part, but as it were a mere shade of the betrayed nymph. He had never dealt with a lady so devoid of coyness and so biddable, and supposed her to be one of Yates's actresses. As he tossed the folds of lace hither and thither about her he knew she would need a mere couple of rehearsals to teach her the rest of the part; and what a relief she was after the stormy German *diva* who took the part of Bertalda!

At home, Decima was eager to tell her father and mother about Caroline's brilliance, but meanwhile her uncle Mr Bertram—that is Sir Thomas Bertram—had walked in and as usual no one else had a chance to speak. Her mother could ask only: 'Where is Caroline now?' and Decima told her: 'Oh, she has gone back to her sewing—you see, in the play, there is a fountain—'

'Is that Stein's piece of Teutonic tosh you refer to?' took up their guest. 'I shall go, I expect. I was invited. But about that, John, you must listen to me: I have some excellent news for you. We are in the way to get hold of enough money for the Orion!'

Decima rose, saying: 'Will you excuse me, please,' and left the room. She was not in the habit of attending her parents' business discussions but in this instance she hoped to make plain to Mr—Sir Thomas—Bertram that any excellent news he brought was not worthy of her interest.

John Yates too was regarding his friend

without perceptible curiosity. 'And what is that?'

'I am taking the worthy and gentlemanly step of closing a feud that has lasted for years between my family—whose head I now am—and another.'

'I am sure that is commendable. What family is the other?'

'Just yesterday, in Bond Street, I happened to meet our old friend James Rushworth.'

'Who is he?'

'You must remember. You met him at Mansfield. After which, he married my sister—and Julia's, Maria. Then when she ran away with some other scoundrel, he divorced her.'

Julia, at this, threw a swift glance at the door of the room to ensure that Decima had closed it firmly behind her.

'Yes,' said John without expression.

'Well, it occurred to me, half way along Bond Street, that our fatuous brother-in-law must be remarkably *rich*.'

'You think so?'

'Certain of it. He had that vast place at Sotherton—grander than our humble acres at Mansfield Park. He still has that house in Wimpole Street. And his doddering mother lives, I'm sure in luxury, in Bath. We dare not mention the name of Rushworth among us and without doubt mother and son scorn to speak the name of Bertram. So yesterday, suddenly it struck me that all that sort of thing is so unnecessary. I embraced him tenderly and said: "Dear James, let us forget the past and be brothers again!" and I invited him to this ballroom farce of Stein's. Now I want you both to be very kind to him and wave the olive branch.'

'Has he not remarried?' Julia enquired.

'I forgot to ask. But who would have him? I promise you—he is still interested in the theatre.'

'You remembered to ascertain that.'

'Now John, do not be sharp with me. I have prepared the ground for you and you should be thankful. Invite him to one of your grand dinner parties to meet a few famous actors and you will gain his notice. As you remember, he was the most dense and boring oaf in the world, but he is longing to be amused, I could see.'

'You do not run to dinner parties or to actors in your own house?' suggested Julia.

'Indeed I could, but just now I cannot afford to be too lavish. There is the question of my having to go to Jamaica and see to matters there. And the travel expenses for that are monstrous.'

'If you are hinting that we furnish monstrous expenses to remove you to the West Indies,' observed John, 'do not imagine that we are not tempted.'

Tom was more hurt than offended. 'I thought I was putting you on to a good thing,'

37

he said, pouting. 'When one's own family turns down an offer of help, what is one to think!'

They had no advice to offer him on this point, and nor did they feel compelled to thank him for helping them to someone else's money. Nor, in addition, did John and Julia regret the passing of James Rushworth out of their lives so many years ago. The rift between the Bertrams and the Rushworths was complete; although the Sotherton estate of James Rushworth was a mere ten miles distant from Mansfield Park. The Yateses had been so rarely at Mansfield that they had not kept up with local tidings or gossip. They may have caught sight of Rushworth in town, but their circles of friends did not intersect, and Rushworth was not a man to attract attention, in any form.

James Rushworth at forty was little different from himself at twenty-five: He was a heavy, sober man of small intelligence and slow speech, and was still under the sway of his mother, who from her house in Bath directed his affairs, summoning him thither and despatching him to Sotherton so that he could rarely settle in his town house and amused himself at theatre or club. He had few friends and his mother had by now apparently wearied of trying to make him find a wife. James could not see that it was necessary to marry, or even to provide an heir for his properties. His first marriage had in any case been engineered by his mother and an aunt of Maria Bertram's and James had entered on it obediently; he did not see how he could have prevented Maria's running away with a man much more handsome and witty than himself; he would readily have admitted, had anyone asked him: 'I suppose I was too dull for her.' Such virtues as he had—such as modesty or generosity— were not those that shine; he seemed contented to remain the dutiful son and to take life as it came. He was much surprised that Tom Bertram accosted him in Bond Street and invited him to some kind of a concert, but did not wonder why.

He did not know the Steins, but was not ill at ease in the grandeur of their house and company; he never felt required to make any sparkling social impression, knowing that people did not expect that of him anyway. He stood about watching the throng, until his long-lost brother Tom Bertram approached crying: 'Ha! Rushworth! Come, you must sit by us. Julia and John are wanting to see you. Julia, this is James—you remember him—'

Greetings on neither side were effusive, but the performance was about to begin and James need do no more than bow to the Yateses and their daughter before taking his chair beside them. It was too late now to recollect that this was Maria's sister; what would his mother say? Well, he must keep it from her that he was fraternising with the forbidden Bertrams, but how he disliked keeping anything from his mother . . . These considerations prevented his devoting attention to the play, and very little could he make of it anyway; he did not know the story, or understand why the *prima donna* need sing in German and so *loudly*, nor why the very thin lady need drift to and fro in the background looking anguished. To this figure, however, he took a great fancy. She was *quiet* and she wore a gown of pale green shimmering material that flowed like water—Well, of course; he had grasped that she was a water sprite; perhaps they were always thin? She was as light as a fairy. By the last scene, James was enjoying himself. Why the bellowing German insisted on having the large stone removed he had no idea, but when the men in Mr Stein's livery (and why not? They were servants to a castle) dragged aside the stone and a jet of foaming white sprang up, breaking from those slender arms to reveal the sprite, James was so delighted with surprise that he laughed aloud.

The Yates daughter spun round to him, hissing angrily: 'It isn't supposed to be funny!'

Totally abashed, James sat blushing and helpless. How to explain—he had not meant that anything was comical—Nor would this fierce young lady listen to him—One or two murmurs of mirth had followed from among the audience—Were they laughing at *him*? The almost immediate end of the performance at least freed him to turn to Tom, who was so affable and might give moral support—and plead:

'What a fool I am—I did not mean—that is, I know not what to say—But I must make my apologies to the lady—the water sprite—Have the goodness to present me—Who is she?'

'Oh Julia's sewing-maid,' Tom told him, not unreasonably after what he had heard Decima say once. 'Apologies for what? Never mind— Come along—' The cast was leaving the stage as the applause died and Tom thrust his way to them saying: 'Allow me, ma'am, to present James Rushworth who wishes to apologize for something—' He did not give her name, which he did not know, but strode away again leaving James face to face with the lady and in greater embarrassment than ever. He gazed at her mute; she gave him her hand and said smiling:

'Thank you, sir, but nor do I know why you should apologize. My name is Caroline Blake. I hope you enjoyed our play.' She could not but be aware of his confusion and pity it, as he found some voice and babbled about laughing—when?—If it was he who had laughed as she emerged from the fountain she could not blame him—she gave him a warmer smile; and James was silenced anew by her sweetness and kindness and the beauty of her unveiled face; he was, to his non-comprehending astonishment, attacked by the symptoms of love.

41

CHAPTER SIX

Caroline felt that by now she must have attempted at least to come 'face to face' with every publisher in London, which she took as a part of the promise to her mother. Until now she had received regrets, denials, refusals polite or peremptory, but it was the publisher who had mentioned payment for his professional services who gave her the first practical advice.

'Listen to me,' began this brisk young Mr Taplow. 'There is a simpler way of going about this than by sewing and ruining your eyes and finger-ends at about seventy stitches for one penny. This is what we should do. You have relations and friends; your brother had friends; we invite them to subscribe in memory of your brother to a small book of selected poems—a *bonne bouche*, handsomely prepared, of the shorter poems—the earlier ones, the country lyrics, and the most appealing; we hold back the classical odes, and the drama, till he has roused enough interest to publish anything further. Now you lay down your needle and compose persuasive letters to all whom you consider his well-wishers—They could not in decency send less than a guinea apiece ... If they send more, it can be laid by for later publications. Then, when we have—fifty guineas, shall we say? I will draw up a choice of poems, and consult you for your own choice, and we shall have a slender book in excellent taste, with gold lettering on a dark green cover—possibly with a few decorative little illustrations—in the first place we might have a small printing of . . . one hundred? Two hundred . . . copies?'

His enthusiasm mounted as he spoke, but he had lost Caroline as soon as he stated the price, and she gazed at him in despair.—Oh, but what he proposed was exactly what she wanted—what she *must* have. Tears flowed. Mr Taplow knew what she felt and added nothing to his speech. He was himself much taken with the image of the slender green-and-gold volume—'Moorland Songs' as a title, for instance? But fair was fair, business was business, and he also sensed the passionate purpose in this young lady; she would be best left alone in her predicament.

Alone Caroline was, but she was aware of that in a fresh sense. Friends? Of course Stephen had had friends; everyone loved him. But she could think of no one whom she could ask for even a guinea. Her grandfather? It was strange that, in escaping from the manor at Dundyke, she and Stephen had left behind all that part of their lives. He had had friends at Cambridge but they were probably all scholarship-poor; and at school—she remembered now the village school and its schoolmaster Mr Piper. He had been fond of Stephen and kind to him. She would begin by consulting Mr Piper. She would certainly not hint that she wanted money, but perhaps he would know whether Mr Taplow's price was fair, and advise her in general. She needed a friend, and wrote with some comfort to herself if no positive hope.

She received none. Mr Piper replied to her letter quickly and affectionately but his news was not reassuring. He had not been in touch with her since Stephen's death and his condolences on that—now he at last had an address for her—were sincere and touching. He said nothing of her plan of publishing Stephen's work except to wish it success; he wrote chiefly about her grandfather.

'. . . I went to visit Mr Holroyd, thinking he might be glad to know I had heard from you. I was not welcomed. I am afraid he has changed recently and is growing into a bitter and lonely old man. Try to understand, my dear, what an unhappy life his has been. You are the last of his family now and he affects to blame you for stealing Stephen away from him. I need not comment on this, nor do I feel it would be wise of you to approach him. Forgive me for telling you this, but he is determined that a young lady alone in London must in order to provide for herself descend to unvirtuous means. He is quite unreasonable and the worse for being spoken to. But I will visit him sometimes although I am not presuming to soften him.

'I am glad to have heard from you because one topic has arisen that I feel I should warn you of: He tells me that in default of your mother and Stephen, you are liable for the debt incurred for Stephen's education. As you will realise from Sedbergh to Cambridge, this has amounted to a considerable sum. Now, can you tell me whether a formal contract was drawn up for this loan, or was it merely a threat he uttered in one of his rages? I am sure you have never admitted any responsibility, but if he were to take any legal action about it you should be prepared . . .'

He ended with good wishes and some local news and the hope of hearing from her again. Caroline was sure of a friend, but not encouraged by the weight of a large—and unjust?—debt added to her poverty. She could only hope that Mr Piper would withhold her address should her grandfather demand it.

She could see that persuasive letters such as Mr Taplow advised must be sent out in quantity, both in order to reach that total amount, and to avoid personal pleas. Her mother, born and brought up at Dundyke, had had friends there, insofar as that isolated and unhospitable house permitted them, but Caroline could suppose that if her grandfather were now putting it about the neighbourhood that his granddaughter had sunk into disrepute in London, it might be useless to approach any of those righteous country dwellers. And as for her own father—and Stephen's—that quiet clergyman whom neither could remember: If he had any family surviving, his children had heard nothing of them.

So she was alone as ever, but a little more resolute now that she had an objective—even if unattainable—and that the weather of London was cooler as the high summer passed, and that she was fully accepted in the Marylebone household, and had had a glimpse of the town's social and artistic life during the Ondine affair. Were she ever to mingle with the Steins—were she ever to make acquaintance with fifty such ... she was not positively hopeful but would not let gleams of daydream ward off despair.

Decima had by now made a great friend of Caroline and would even follow her up to her room and sit chattering while Caroline worked. Cheerful company on a rainy morning did Caroline no harm; nor had the sustenance and surroundings of this house, after her previous privations. Her needle flew. Only now and then Decima's prattle would touch on the future in a way that was a little disturbing:

'... And I should be "out" by Christmas but Papa wonders whether I should wait until the year's mourning for my grandfather is up—I hope not. I could not bear it. And Mama says we ought to go down to Mansfield Park soon, for another visit. At least my Uncle Tom says so. But it is so dull in the country. Nor is he at all often there himself; after all she is *his* mother . . .'

'Who is?' asked Caroline, puzzled, as Decima paused for a deep sigh. It was not always easy to follow Decima's meaning, when a delicate piece of stitching must be achieved.

'Well you know, my grandmother. Lady Bertram. Will she be the Dowager Lady Bertram when Uncle Tom marries, or Elizabeth Lady Bertram—indeed I do not know if that is her given name. No, of course, she is Maria, but that is a name no one speaks of nowadays in the family. Were I to tell you of the scandalous history of our family—which I am not supposed to know—you would be horrified.' She observed that Caroline did not seem to be attending, and took this as a reproach for family disloyalty, and sighing again, desisted.

Caroline had been mildly horrified by the recollection that she herself had no part in family life except as chaperone to Decima and that with Decima visiting her grandmother— 'out' in society—in no need of surveillance— Caroline would be redundant. What rather surprised her as she recognised that, was her own feeling of loss. She had grown fond of Decima. Here was a real friend, of a kind Caroline had not had before.

After this, she began to talk more, and to confide in Decima; Decima knew already that

Caroline was working to save enough money for the publication of her late brother's poetry, but the tale of Mr Taplow and his fifty guineas added to her interest. Decima had never been concerned with money apart from what she could spend on herself, and she saw Caroline's position as similar to her father's over the acquisition of the Orion theatre; what a pity it was that people should not have enough money for what they wanted. She had understood that it was her Uncle Tom who was not giving her father some money he had promised, but no one was evidently withholding help from Caroline, whose confidences did not extend to include her grandfather. Decima's admiration for Caroline increased as she calculated the years it might take, even with Caroline's industry, to produce fifty guineas' worth of fine needlework—the more so as Caroline did not appear dismayed by the reckonings, but stitched on with steady purpose.

What else, Caroline wondered, could she do? She might as well stitch on as not, while the rain fell and life was dull after the Ondine adventure.

One after-effect of that episode had, Decima averred, rendered the house duller than before: Mr James Rushworth had taken to calling. He had nothing to say; he wanted nothing.

Morning calls were not normally a part of

James Rushworth's life when he was in Wimpole Street, and it was a normal feature of his life that he had nothing to say. His own boldness alarmed him when he set out on the pretext of thanking the Yateses for his invitation to 'Ondine'—forgetting that it was Tom Bertram who had invited him; as for his sub-pretext, that he might see the sewing-maid, he knew it would be unrewarded. But once starting a course of action he did not know how to abandon it; he called again, and on the seventh (Decima thought) occasion he encountered Caroline in the hallway with Decima, was re-introduced, rendered completely dumb, but was all the more committed to the romantic bondage that had held him since the evening of the water sprite; he was dumb and dazed, and could only compound this by calling again on the next morning.

On this morning Julia, looking out of her boudoir window at the rain, stepped quickly back saying: 'Oh—here is Mr Rushworth *again* ... I cannot bear it. Decima, do you receive him; I must begin my letters.' Decima, trying on necklaces, gave one of her sighs and Julia added: 'I would ask Caroline but I know she has just gone up to start her work—'

'Very well, then, for her sake I will grant him an audience of five and a half minutes.' And Decima ran down to the drawingroom, depriving James of a confrontation with

Caroline but to conduct a five and a half minute conversation that was to have some effect. She assured him in turn that each member of the household was well; '—and is Miss Blake well?'

'Yes, I thank you, Mr Rushworth. She is busy just now with her own work.'

'You do not mean, with sewing?' asked James, who had not yet quite understood his Ondine's status in the household.

'She sews, but for a good reason,' said Decima, pursuing from some teasing spirit: 'Do you care much for poetry, Mr Rushworth?'

'Poetry? I? No, I cannot do with the stuff. I can never understand it,' said James simply and without regret. Decima threw up her hands exclaiming:

'Well, whatever you do, do not say so to Caroline. She is very fond of it and she had a brother who died and was a poet, and she cares about his poetry more than anything in the world.'

James frowned anxiously. 'You do not suppose,' he ventured after a moment, 'that she would expect me to read poems?' Decima laughed at his discomfiture but said:

'Perhaps not, but her brother's poems she will expect all the world to read as soon as they are published!'

'Published: Do you mean, printed and made into a book?'

'I believe that is what the word "published"

usually means,' said the naughty Decima. Then she repented, and lest he should notice that she was mocking him, continued on the subject: 'And, you see, she is so poor, and is trying to save up so that she can pay a man with a name like Tadpole—a publisher, but the shocking thing is that he wants fifty guineas from her.' She glanced at the clock: Five minutes gone. Mr Rushworth did not look at all shocked by her information but was staring at her as if he were not listening. So she rose, filled in thirty seconds with formal thanks to him for his call, rang for the servant to show him out, and ran upstairs again to her necklaces.

When for the next two days there was no sign of Mr Rushworth Decima began to suffer twinges of conscience: Had she offended him? Perhaps the rain had prevented his coming. But on the following day when it rained more heavily, Julia and John were still in the breakfast room—it was early—a servant announced:

'Mr Rushworth is at the door, sir, and he wishes to speak to Miss Blake.'

'At this hour? Show him up to the drawingroom, Wilkins—'

'He says he cannot wait, sir.'

'Then find Miss Blake for him, by all means, and bring her down,' commanded John, more concerned with his eggs. Caroline, surprised, followed Wilkins to the front hallway where

Mr Rushworth stood silent and wet. Before she had bidden him good morning he stepped forward and thrust at her a folded paper; it was as wet as he, but when she unfolded it, it was dry enough for her to read; it was not the legibility but the purport that struck her: She held a note of hand for the sum of fifty guineas.

He stared at her under his eyebrows and muttered: 'For your brother.' Her face had turned white and she stared back at him, blindly. She could not speak. Nor could he; he turned away, clapping his wet hat on to his head, opening the door for himself and striding out into the downpour.

Caroline made her way to the breakfast room where she knew Mr Yates to be, holding out to him the paper as if she wished him to translate it to her. He observed her state of shock, read the document aloud, slowly, then said as he passed it to his wife: 'This is quite in order, my dear. You look as if you cannot believe it, but this sum is yours to spend as you wish.'

Caroline shook her head, incredulous; Julia taking it for denial said; 'But you will accept it: You do not feel you should return it to Mr Rushworth?'

'Oh no; I could not do that,' Caroline replied with cool decision. Indeed she did not apply Mr Rushworth's action to herself. The money was for Stephen; Mr Rushworth had said so, too. She had not thought of thanking him and he had invited no thanks. Julia was watching her with a touch of curiosity; she had always sensed this streak of what she would call hardness in Caroline, who in her private life was single-minded to the point of being single-hearted; and yet, thought Julia as she had before, one has to respect her. She said in a motherly tone: 'But you will write to thank Mr Rushworth, will you not?'

A shudder seemed to quiver through Caroline as if an unseemly suggestion had been made to her, and John Yates, perceptive when his mind could be engaged, said: 'I think that in the case of a gift of this size there must be a formal acknowledgement. I shall write to Mr Rushworth on Caroline's behalf, expressing her gratitude if she wishes me to, but making it clear that you and I are privy to the whole transaction and that any further approaches he may wish to make to Caroline will be under our scrutiny.'

Caroline, folding her drying paper, paid no heed to this, but Julia reflected that John too had treated the matter with becoming seriousness besides being very kind to Caroline—whom he often nowadays addressed as 'my dear'. What he could mean by 'further approaches' that stupid Mr Rushworth might make towards Caroline one could not imagine; surely Caroline could take good care of herself. This point of view was soon shown by

Decima, who now ran into the breakfast room with her hair half curled, crying: 'What are you all doing? Was that Mr Rushworth I saw, tramping away in the rain? I thought you had asked him to breakfast and what a strange thing to do—' So she must see the evidence of Mr Rushworth's astonishing gift, which she greeted with a delight all the greater since *she* had brought it about—Who else had told him about the fifty guineas? She felt it wiser however not to claim any credit: as to Mr Rushworth's motives, she cared not at all about them as long as Caroline got her money; though at the back of her mind she, at a romantic age, might have devised something of his feeling for Caroline—his Ondine, his *Belle dame sans merci*, his ideal—had he not been a dull old man of about forty.

CHAPTER SEVEN

Caroline made all haste to tell Mr Taplow of her sudden affluence. Mr Taplow was much surprised, which Caroline did not notice; her good fortune was already assumed. She did not understand why he detained her with offers of wine and general conversation; he had sent out privily to confirm the existence of this Rushworth and his circumstances. This done, he twirled a pen and blinked at his client and murmured:

'This benefactor... He is perhaps a relative? An uncle...?'

'I met him only a few weeks ago.'

'He is very generous then.'

'When do you expect the book to be printed?' urged Caroline, keeping to essentials.

'Ah... Well now...' A young woman who could obtain such a sum of money so promptly had hidden resources. He might have under-rated her. Lying back in his chair he began: 'There will be a great deal of work, the editing and format and binding... And even now, you know, prices are increasing; if you want a really elegant production, with gold decoration, the overall cost—'

'You *said* fifty guineas,' she reminded him in a voice that showed him he had not under-rated her. Lamenting that his entire business would be ruined if he ever again gave an unknown writer such terms as these, he resigned himself and agreed to submit all the poems immediately to an experienced editor on his staff, and as a privilege to let Miss Blake see the editor's version before the printing was undertaken. Caroline, who had indeed expected nothing else, was reluctant; how long, she asked, would the editor take? Ah well, said Mr Taplow, it rather depended on how much other work he at present had in hand...

Caroline was inexperienced in dealing with

publishers, but that she was now dealing with one indicated that her cause was in a way to be gained, and she was happier than had seemed possible. She let Decima draw her from the endless sewing for a while, and they walked in the park as the rain eased, or visited Decima's friends to play whist and to talk about clothes. 'Caroline can be quite frivolous,' Decima told her mother.

'Let us hope it will continue.'

There was little frivolity among the others of the family. John Yates, preparing to write to Mr Rushworth on Caroline's account, had remarked to his wife: 'We must not tell your brother Sir Thomas about this lavishness of Rushworth's. If you remember, it was we whom he intended to profit from it, and not Caroline.' But Tom had to be told; in fact he took it well, pointing out that fifty guineas was nothing to a man of Rushworth's means, and that it proved how ready he was with his money in a good cause. 'I do not know why I should not put it to him direct,' Tom protested. 'Especially since we heard that Italian brigand has put in an offer for the Orion that is higher than ours.' Higher than John Yates's, he should have said: Tom was no nearer to settling his father's affairs, letting Mansfield Park, or departing for Antigua. Dropping into the Yateses' house he noticed Caroline for the first time; he had not hitherto observed her large and striking eyes or her delicate figure;

56

he had thought her a skinny little creature, if the truth were known, and his judgement may not have been influenced by his new view of her as the recipient of good fortune; Caroline, happier, had taken on a happier appearance altogether.

During these days, nothing was heard from Mr Rushworth. No one gave him much thought; he had as it were shot his bolt, made his dramatic gesture, and sunk back into obscurity. This was very much what James had intended; he was in a glow of satisfaction that he had paid his tribute to his demi-goddess without any 'fuss'. He might even have called again at the Yateses' once they had seen that he wanted no 'fuss' or thanks; for a few days he rested in the luxury of feeling pleased with himself but then an event occurred that interrupted his peace: The unheralded arrival of his mother.

Mrs Rushworth was of about the same age as Lady Bertram but they were of different temperaments. Even during the few years of the marriage of the latter to the son of the former they had formed no friendship. Indeed they had rarely met, although they lived only ten miles apart in the country.

Mrs Rushworth was a worrier. Every mishap presaged calamity, and she pointed this out as if she would feel justified when disaster struck. She had no high opinion of the abilities or intentions of her son and only child James, who could never be persuaded to worry; to his mother, he was still a lazy, heedless, unsympathetic boy. On this occasion he listened (or did he?) to her complaints with a silly half-smile on his face. He took nothing seriously.

It was true that James had a struggle to assemble his wits (never a rapid process) and remember who last wrote to whom, and about what, and what his mother wanted of him now. It was as if he had forgotten about her, and saw her through the mental mist of his private happiness. One familiar topic arose:

'It troubles me so much that you remain in this house after all you suffered here. You should not be constantly reminded of Maria—'

'I never think about Maria,' James assured her, smiling broadly.

Her suspicious glance said: Well, you should. 'It is too lonely for you. You will never marry unless you meet the right people—'

'I might not in any case.'

'That, I cannot bear to hear. There must be an heir to Sotherton. Your father set so much store by it. What if your father himself had shirked marriage? What would you have thought of him?'

'Had he done so,' said James after thinking it over, 'I should not have been born to have any opinion.'

This may have been the intellectual level attained in her discussions with her son, but

Mrs Rushworth admitted that he was not clever; nor did she regret that, since he was honest and upright and led a virtuous life, which was more important; his simple mind may have made him more tractable; that he should deceive or defy her was quite unthinkable.

She was the more incredulous when, on her first morning in Wimpole Street she as usual bade James bring her his household books on the usual pretext (though none was required by James) of making sure no one was cheating him, she beheld the entry of fifty guineas paid out to a Miss Blake.

'*What* can this mean?'

The honest James so habitually kept his books correctly to show to his mother that he had not foreseen that she would read this entry. Looking at his mother's pointing finger he was at a loss. He explained: 'You see, I paid that amount to Miss Blake', but had to recognise that it was not much of an explanation.

'*Who* is Miss Blake?'

'She is a lady who needed some money.'

'*Why* did she need money?'

'It is for her brother's poems. He died.'

'And what have *you* to do with poets?'

'Nothing, ma'am. He is dead.'

Mrs Rushworth removed her eyeglasses and fixed on him a more glacial stare. 'And how came you to meet this Miss Blake?'

James recollected now that he had met Miss Blake through Tom Bertram in the first place, which would be quite unacceptable to his mother. In catching himself back from that indiscretion he sounded hesitant as he muttered awkwardly: 'I saw her on a stage—It was some kind of a play—'

'An *actress*!' cried Mrs Rushworth utterly horrified. This seemed to be the worst that could happen—or if not, she was bound according to her nature to make the worst of it. Her *son*—becoming entangled with an actress—immoral women all—behind his mother's back—and squandering large sums of money upon her—Mrs Rushworth's voice rose almost to a shriek as she enlarged upon James's foolishness, cowardice, depravity and her own despair of him. He once or twice tried to insert: 'No, you see, it is not like that—' but had to allow the tirade to engulf him. It was only as his mother in peroration turned to the practical that he became uneasy.

'You must leave London at once. You will come with me directly to Sotherton, where you have not been for some time, occupied as you are with the disgraceful pursuit of your base pleasures. We shall set out early tomorrow. And when you are living as the country gentleman you are supposed to be, that will be the end of your shameful secret life.'

Leave town? That was so far from his desire that he did not protest. Nor did he engage in his mother's description of his life style. As practical as she, he told her: 'Tomorrow I have an appointment with the gunsmith. And I must visit the vintner's.'

She looked at him, checked by surprise. Did she sense that he was not truly ashamed—that his 'secret life' was his true life and unassailable? She at any rate did not force the issue but she remembered that she had come to London largely to consult a physician said to be more knowledgeable than any in Bath, about the rheumatism in her wrist. One day's delay might be afforded; she was certain that when she had him settled at Sotherton, all the nonsense about actresses would be forgotten and his life of deceit would be over.

James however could quite calmly assume that a life of deceit was beginning. His mother had overstated her case: Talk of immoral women and shameful life clearly had no relevance to Miss Blake or to his feeling for her. What he must do, only, was to let her know that he was to leave London—this, his mother was right about; he was normally at Sotherton at this time of year and his presence was necessary. He knew that. He did not even care whether he found Miss Blake at home this morning; her image was secure. As he set out, deceitfully, for the Yateses' house instead of for the gunsmith's he was unusually cool-headed and further cool ideas occurred to him: I am glad that I met Tom Bertram again and I do not see why we were not to meet. After all, *I* am the person who was the sufferer—the wronged husband. And if I want to be friends with the Bertrams what stupid convention is it that keeps us apart? I do not see why I should not choose my own friends, at my age.

Mrs Yates was the only one at home, but she received him as if she were pleased to see him; James's diffidence had not let him see that she was not, previously; but today she was in a sunny humour and had happy news:

'What do you think, Mr Rushworth—We are truly to have the Orion after so long! The Italian buyer backed out—some quarrel with the owner—and John has acquired a new partner who will make up the price! It is Mr Stein—you remember him? He had no idea that John was in need of money and wishes he had offered before to help—'

James had not been made aware, either, of the difficulty, or had not understood it. He thought now: But I would have liked to offer some money, had I been asked—Though what would my mother have said about *that*? And Julia thought: And you, my friend are fortunate that Tom had not yet approached you; you might have been tempted to munificence on the scale of yours to Caroline, and I cannot see you as a man of the theatre. She smiled at his congratulations, and went on:

'So John is in good heart again, and will be busy, so—this I must tell you—I shall feel free to visit my mother again to cheer her mourning a little. I shall take Decima with me, and Caroline too. She will be company for Decima and she needs a change of air; she is still having trouble I believe about her brother's book and its publication. And she will I am sure like to see Mansfield Park.'

Mansfield Park! James's heart gave a leap. An hour's ride from Sotherton on a fresh horse . . . ! His voice sounded husky as he said:

'I too am leaving town. I called this morning to say goodbye. I am going with my mother to Sotherton. You remember Sotherton?'

'Very well,' said Julia, laughing. 'So it may not be goodbye; we can meet in Northamptonshire—although my mother is still not in spirits for visiting; and yours—She will not be willing for us to plague her?'

'I do not see why not,' cried James, adding hastily: 'Not that you—anyone—I do not mean plague—'

'It is absurd, I agree, that we should not all be on good terms after so long. You yourself have been a very good friend to Caroline, for instance.' She mentioned this with a touch of impishness, amused by her guest's response to the sound of that name; and James blushed again as he took up:

'Yes, please, you must tell me why there is trouble about the book. Does the publisher want any more money, for instance?'

'I do not believe so. It is something about

63

the editing of the poems, Decima tells me. But you must ask Caroline about it yourself.'

'I would not dare. I know nothing of poetry.'

'Then it was the more generous of you to help her as you did. She is a tenacious young woman,' added Julia in a confidential tone, 'and I feel she cares more about those poems than about anything in the world. I find it extraordinary.'

'I do not,' asserted James stoutly. 'She is loyal to her brother and I admire it.'

'Yes, of course,' conceded Julia. She liked to see the dull Mr Rushworth scarlet-faced and puffed up about something he admittedly did not understand, and she was glad for Caroline to have so fervent an ally, and wished she thought Caroline would appreciate it.

CHAPTER EIGHT

Caroline had written to Mr Taplow, asking whether he had yet decided on a publication date for Stephen's poems, and Mr Taplow replied that the editor's work was already half completed, and that he would be happy should Miss Blake visit his office to see what had been achieved and to give it her approval.

She had not understood what was meant by 'editing' and was much taken aback when Mr Taplow laid before her on his desk, with some flourish, her tidy manuscript sheets apparently attacked by a red pen and great speed, and sprinkled with question marks, crossing-out, scrawled words, and illegible figures in every corner. She gazed at the pages helplessly.

'But .. What was wrong with it all . . .?'

'Oh not wrong, ma'am—Nothing is *wrong*. It is just that the editor—a man of considerable experience—thought some small modifications would make the work more accessible to the general reader. When you have studied them I am sure you will agree.'

Somehow Caroline was afraid she would not. Puzzled, she lifted the uppermost sheet, obediently studied that, and asked: 'Why has the editor crossed out this word—for instance . . .?' All the poems were so familiar to her that it almost felt like a desecration to spatter Stephen's words with cruel red ink.

'May I see . . . Ah yes; perhaps that is a little too unusual—" . . . The skirling curlew . . ."'

'In the north, we speak of "skirling" pipes—'

'Pipes? I cannot allow that a curlew sounds like a bagpipe.'

'Not *sounds* like one; *skirls* like one.' He stared at her, failing to see the distinction. 'The "singing curlew" is comparatively meaningless here. Almost any bird can *sing*. And besides— we need the word as the internal rhyme, three lines lower, for "Whirling".'

Mr Taplow regarded the lines with polite non-comprehension. He had expected the lady to object to the editor's changes—all writers did—but he had not expected such a detailed and determined attack. After all, these poems had not been written by the lady herself. He underestimated the ferocity with which Caroline might defend the work just because it was not hers, but Stephen's.

He could recognise however the cool authority with which Miss Blake was turning the pages before her, and he quailed at the supposition that she would take him line by line through the lot—and there was the other half to follow. He addressed her:

'You will understand, I am sure, Miss Blake, that the editor—and I—are anxious to help you. We make these suggestions with your interests at heart—for your own good. Perhaps you are not—coming from the north—acquainted with the literary tastes and fashions of the metropolis. There may be in these poems some over-simplicity—some small rusticities—'

'My brother was a rustic boy,' she said, indifferently.

'Quite so. One can perceive that—'

'But you still have perceived in the latter part of my manuscript that he wrote sonnets at Cambridge, and I also have his last work, a verse drama—'

'I do earnestly beg you to reconsider very carefully before you ask me to publish this material in disregard of expert advice—'

'Mr Taplow,' she said, glancing up at him, still coolly, 'who may I ask you is paying for the publication?'

'Ah well. Yes. But let us not become merely commercial-minded.' Nevertheless she had a point there. Mr Taplow had not yet read her sonnets; in all he might not lose on the publication. He smiled in relief, saying:

'Well now, shall we see if we can come to a temporary and useful arrangement? I would like you to take those corrected pages away with you and consider them very carefully.' It must be remembered that Mr Taplow's editor had put a good deal of time, work and red ink into the project and even if he lacked poetic sense, must be pacified. 'When you have written out a fresh version, with or without his or your amendments, we will begin modifications of what is to be the latter part of the book, but it is better to have all parties satisfied.'

She seemed to be, for the moment, acquiescent, though his plan did not amount to much. She was doubtful only because she was soon leaving London for a visit to Northamptonshire, of unknown length; but he assured her: 'There are always the postal services, ma'am!' and bade her farewell with great goodwill. Let her go skirling off into the Midlands and allow him some respite.

Caroline, making her way back to Marylebone, might have felt, had her

67

imagination been of a morbid nature, that she bore away the body of Stephen stained by arrow stabs; but she also felt, in fancy or fact, that the wounds were not deep; her purpose held; she had even gained some advantage in this skirmish with the world of publishing. She was not distracted by an encounter with Decima's uncle Sir Thomas who was just descending the steps of the house muttering to himself: '... Of course, they are all at that theatre ...' and gave Caroline a half-bow that she as coolly returned. She was taking no part in the activities stirred up by the acquisition of the Orion—the discussions of acoustics, properties, woodworm in the balcony rails— and she was content to be excluded.

Tom, quite to the contrary, suffered bitterly from his exclusion. What did that *arriviste* Stein know of theatrical affairs? How could the venture succeed without Tom's expertise and taste? Worse—his own sister was siding with the lawyers in threatening to exclude him from his own house. They all pointed out that if Tom were to give up his London house and live at Mansfield Park, the saving would be considerable. 'And with such a saving,' Julia pointed out, 'we might be able to give up the idea of letting the Park; and our mother can be left in peace there.'

Tom had not yet accepted any idea of letting the Park, nor of himself settling to the life of a country squire, but he could not protest the matter were his mother's peace in question. He felt that banishment was being thrust upon him—almost, that everyone was against him, that everyone else had the good luck. He was not petty-minded enough to resent this Miss Blake—the little sewing-maid who had somehow been established as one of the Yates family—for her luck in acquiring money from Rushworth; the more fool Rushworth and Tom wished her joy of it—but it did not raise his spirits when even Miss Blake virtually 'cut' him on the doorsteps of the Marylebone house. Well he was going down tomorrow to Mansfield himself as it happened, to share the peace of the happy country-dwellers in Northamptonshire; these lucky town-dwellers could amuse themselves as they wished in his absence, which they probably would not notice.

His spirits did not improve when he found Mansfield just as usual—as it had lately been—when he arrived in squally autumn weather that prohibited even riding about the country; his mother sat with her needlework and pugs, now wearing her grey gowns of half-mourning; Susan awaited him in his father's office room with ledgers to be studied and bills to be paid; boredom made him sigh aloud as he stood by the hearth, teasing one of the pugs with the toe of his boot. He supposed he should talk to his mother but could think of nothing to say. The morning was dark and windy. A fierce gust sent twigs and dead leaves rattling along the windows, rather startling Tom, who was more startled when Lady Bertram suddenly threw down her work and cried with an uncharacteristic passion:

'Oh Tom—How I *dread* the winter!' This broke from her with a burst of tears that alarmed him. He said awkwardly:

'This is not yet winter. It is only autumn—'

Inattentive, his mother sobbed, her hands over her face: 'The evenings, the long evenings when Sir Thomas read aloud—The dark—And he played solitaire with Susan—Or she would play the pianoforte to him . . . We were so happy . . . So peaceful . . .'

Tom could imagine that the absence of Sir Thomas would make a significant difference to the happiness of this small domestic circle. He was touched, and disturbed, by grief and woe such as he had not witnessed before in his mother. Still awkwardly he said:

'Please do not cry so. I will—' What? He fell back on the recourse of a man faced with deep feminine feeling: '—I will bring Susan to you—'

He fled to his father's office room where Susan, smooth and calm as ever, was writing in one of her ledgers. Tom appealed to her:

'My mother is upset—distressed—Could you offer her any comfort?'

'Could not *you* do so?' she returned; then observing his troubled face she asked: 'What is it that has upset her?'

'She dreads the winter evenings . . .'

'That does not surprise me,' remarked Susan, laying down her pen and leaving the room. Tom did not accompany her, but delayed to study the ledgers and repress the image of the winter evenings he himself might expect if he joined the household. What had they done during such evenings when they were children? Some sober reading aloud there had been, but he seemed to remember games and laughter? He was sighing heavily over the dullness of adult life when presently Susan came back, saying:

'She is easier now I think. She has taken some wine.' She took up her pen but pointed it at Tom like a rapier and said in a commanding tone: 'Tom. You know what makes her unhappy, do you not?'

'Yes, of course—My father—'

'Of course. But in addition, it is simply that she is lonely.'

'She has you . . .' began Tom. 'And someone from the Parsonage comes up to see her every day.'

'And she has the pleasure of your company when brighter pleasures do not intervene,' supplied Susan. The sharply pointing pen inhibited his denial. 'Tom, listen to me. You must admit that a house of this size needs people—life—children—in fact, a family.'

As this notion had occurred to him while Susan was out of the room he disclaimed, hotly: 'I do not see that as necessary at all. Indeed the noise of small children would be disturbing to my mother—'

'Then they must be kept out of earshot—or kept quiet,' said Susan, dismissively. 'It should not be impossible. Your objection is merely technical. Do you not, honestly, feel that the house is not *alive*? The nursery and schoolroom are empty—there are no ponies in the stables—no one hammering out scales on that old pianoforte—And I am sure you and Edmund were beaten and sent to bed early often enough, for fighting over your toys—'

'Let us hope such days are past,' said Tom with an attempt at scorn.

'They can recur. All I am insisting on is that there should be a family again. It is your responsibility.'

That irksome word made him flinch. 'And how do you suppose I provide a family?'

Susan was laughing. 'I believe the normal procedure is for a man in the first place to find a lady who meets his requirements to propose marriage to her, and—'

'Yes, yes,' he interrupted, waving a hand. 'I appreciate your wit—and sentiments—on the subject, but I do not wish to marry.'

If he wanted to expand on this, he was prevented by Susan's brisk change of course. 'Your mother was telling me about a ball Sir Thomas once gave for my sister here, and how much she enjoyed it. I know that there cannot be similar festivities here until the spring—not even, I suppose, at Christmas; and that is why I have asked Julia to come again—and bring Decima, and Mortimer when his school term ends—just to have several people in the house—to give it more life; that I am sure would help my aunt. I hope too they will bring Miss Blake, whom I would like to meet—'

'I do not expect you would. She is a chilly creature.'

'Well, but I am interested to meet new people. Did you read this letter from Gibbons and Son, about the Low Farm tenancy?' She handed him the letter but he did not unfold it; he was forming a thought strange to him, and a feeling of shame that it should be so. When did Susan meet new people? How had Susan enjoyed the long dark evenings with Sir Thomas and Lady Bertram? Tom had from time to time admitted to himself that 'we all take Susan for granted' but the thought had stopped there; how, he now wondered, had Susan borne that so cheerfully for so long? He was conscious of a fresh appreciation of Susan; he had not valued her enough. For instance, her strictures on himself—candid and frequently offered—did not annoy him as did the nagging of Julia or the well-phrased advice of his pious brother—Indeed, he felt closer to Susan than to any of his relations or friends, it now struck him; she was determined, but had a lightness of touch—an inability in herself to be

73

injured by anything he said; she did not take him seriously. No—that was not true; but she had a seriousness that held a centre of something like affection.

He said, frowning, with unusual vehemence: 'Why do you *stay* here?'

'Here—at Mansfield? I like to think I am useful,' she said in her light tone with its tinge of irony.

'But can that be enough? It is not only now—It has been going on for years. My mother says she cannot spare you, but you must know she would not wish you to waste—give away—your whole life in being indispensable. You could have travelled—seen more of the world—Even, visited your own mother—'

Susan laughed outright. Did Tom not know that Mrs Price, sister of Lady Bertram, was so grateful to have two of her daughters domiciled at Mansfield Park that she had virtually lost interest in them, being caught up in the affairs of the rest of her over-large family in Portsmouth. When her husband died, at about three years before this time, Sir Thomas had bought for her a neat little cottage in the purlieus of Portsmouth in which she could settle peacefully; but far from that, the Bertrams learnt that the whole pack of her family had pursued her thither, bringing their wives and children between their naval sorties, so that the chaos was often as frightful as in their own rackety childhood.

'What is so amusing in that?' Tom was suspicious.

'I have always been grateful for the peace of Mansfield Park,' Susan said, 'even when it is in sadness. Now please read that letter, and tell me what I am to say in reply.' It was more probable that Susan would tell him, but from long habit Tom obeyed without question. He took Susan for granted still, it was true, but was becoming more sensible of the granting spirit; like his mother, but in his own terms, he did not know what he would do without Susan. He wondered that he had never wondered this before.

CHAPTER NINE

Lady Bertram regained her composure, if not yet fully her spirits, as those first autumn storms blew over and were succeeded by blue skies and the first sparkle of frost. She was, as Susan had hoped, glad to have more company in the house. 'I think,' she told Julia, 'that your friend Miss Blake is a very pleasant and quiet young lady. And I am pleased especially that Tom is to stay longer this time. He is in no hurry to return to town.'

Nor, in truth, was Julia. 'No one in town speaks of anything but that theatre now,' Julia said. 'And I feel a little excluded myself.' She understood that Tom was more offended by his exclusion than she, and was the more surprised that he now spoke of it so lightly. '*Pah*, the Orion,' he exclaimed. 'I have better things to do than to hang about measuring sight-lines. This is the best time of year for being in the country and I mean to enjoy it.' He meant to enjoy some foxhunting; mourning might be ignored for the sake of exercising his horses, though he dutifully wore his black bands.

To Susan he said: 'You see, Susan, how I attend to your wishes. You like fresh people, and here is Miss Blake, a serious and clever lady like yourself. She will be just the friend for you.'

Susan had thought something of the kind already. Serious Miss Blake was, but not companionable. She passed most of her time in the old schoolroom studying and copying the poems of her brother's that were to be published. It was the generous Tom who initiated the closer acquaintance between the two ladies by commanding one morning in the breakfast room:

'Now, Susan, if you are to go down to the Parsonage with those nuts, you must take Miss Blake with you. Julia says she is to have country air, and surely you can tempt her away from her poetry for a half hour.'

Confronted by this confrontation neither

lady refused it; they set off down the park together, talking of the trees and the weather and the uses to which hazel nuts could be put, could they be gathered before the squirrels had done so. Miss Blake described a recipe from her childhood. '—Were you brought up in the country, then? I took you for a Londoner,' Susan said. Her companion replied to this so tersely that it was evident she did not wish to speak about herself. It was not until the visit had been performed and the empty basket was being borne homeward that, in the enforced intimacy of being alone together again, Miss Blake's manner seemed to soften. She asked in an almost confidential tone:

'Am I, won't you tell me, taking too little part in the life of the household? I am very grateful to be here, and I would not like my hosts to think me selfish. Does Sir Thomas want me to go riding? I believe I refused him too abruptly—'

'No, no, you must do just as you please. You are his guest and he would want you to be happy. If,' she could not help adding, 'the work on your brother's poetry does make you happy.'

Miss Blake accepted this readily; she sighed and observed; 'It might not indeed seem to. I will try to be more cheerful . . .' Then as Susan paused, listening, Miss Blake's reserve fell away and she cried: 'I do not know what to *do* about the poems.'

Susan looked astonished inquiry; she sensed that this was the first time Miss Blake had uttered this complaint to anyone, and she did not press for explanations; she hoped that silent sympathy would encourage Miss Blake to continue; and so it did.

'I did not think of this for some time,' Miss Blake hurried on, 'and you see, the editor made so many changes—he *changed* the poems so that in many places they were not Stephen's at all. I knew that was wrong. But then I wondered—Oh, all this is of no interest to you and it would take so long to tell the whole story—'

'I can stand here for the whole day and listen,' said Susan smiling, swinging the empty basket, persuasive. 'Please tell me.'

And so, out poured the story of the debt owed to Grandfather for Stephen's education, of which Stephen had known: '. . . and whether our grandfather is going to law about it as Mr Piper warned me, still Stephen would have wished to repay, at least as much as he could—so if Mr Taplow says the book will not sell unless I accept the editor's changes, ought I to let the book be printed with them, for the sake of Stephen's honour?'

There was some confusion and much anxiety in the recital but Susan could understand Miss Blake's dilemma. 'Certainly not,' she answered, positively. 'You must see that the poems are printed as Stephen wrote them, saleable or not.'

'Do you mean that Stephen himself would put his poetry before his honour?'

'Yes, I do. But, let us put it this way round: Would your brother write poems merely to earn money? You are making him into a literary hack?'

'Oh—not *that!*' exclaimed Miss Blake horrified. She pondered for a moment, then threw up her head and laughed, though tears brimmed in her eyes, while her cheeks flushed. Why, said Susan to herself, how pretty she is! 'Of course you are right,' Miss Blake was saying. 'I cannot tell you how grateful I am.'

'I have said nothing that you did not already know,' Susan told her, also laughing.

'Well, then I am doubly reassured, and doubly thankful.' They resumed their walk in an accord that would have surprised Tom and caused him to marvel at his success in fostering friendships.

After this, Caroline worked on with a freer mind and more courage. She had noted that the 'editor' produced a poetic style of his own modelled on that of Mr Wordsworth she suspected; whatever he thought of Stephen's 'rusticities', was it any improvement to introduce poetisms such as 'e'er' for 'ever' when two syllables were needed, or to replace a simple 'green' with 'verdant'? Her loyalty to Stephen was undisturbed and her resolution refreshed by Susan's ready understanding.

Tom, later on that day, was gratified to find all the ladies gathered peaceably at their work, Miss Blake together at the table with Susan, while Julia stitched beside Lady Bertram and Decima for whom the scene was perhaps a little too industrious read a novel on the far sofa.

'Aha! The little sewing-maid again!' Tom exclaimed. No one asked what he meant; his geniality was appreciated but his motives not examined; it was enough nowadays that he on his side seemed to appreciate so much feminine company. 'How are your poems proceeding, Miss Blake?'

'Well, I thank you. Miss Price has been encouraging me.'

'And so she would. Susan encourages us all.'

'Yes; I could not do without her,' put in Lady Bertram.

'Let us hope you are never required to.'

'I do not see how that could come about,' said his mother in her tranquil fashion.

'No, no. Do not give it a thought. So when your poems are ready, Miss Blake, we may lose you from our little circle?'

'I should be sorry to leave,' Caroline said. 'I have been very fortunate, have I not, in all the help I have been given, since the gift of the money—for which I now feel I was not suitably grateful—'

'Do you speak of Mr Rushworth's gift?' called Decima from her sofa. 'Remember it

80

was I who told him about your difficulty . . .'

A strange silence fell upon the group; Caroline raised her head to see that covert glances were being directed towards Lady Bertram, who said in surprise:

'Mr Rushworth? Of Sotherton? How came you to know him?'

'Oh,' cried Tom, guiltily casual, 'one sees him about town at times. You know how it is . . .'

Lady Bertram drew out her needle and admired the stitch before remarking unhurriedly: 'Sir Thomas did not allow us to speak of him.'

This held no reproof, nor a more than passing interest. 'Susan,' she went on, 'I think I shall use the dark green thread on all the leaves round the edge of the pattern. I think it was a pity that Maria married him at all. And I was thinking; I would like one of these roasted apples for supper.' She held out her needle for Susan to thread, meanwhile studying her work with approbation. Tom, turning his back to her, sent a smile and a roll of his eyes around the company, murmuring: 'Family feud? I fancy it is outdated.'

'Fortunately,' appended Julia, 'since you yourself have already arranged that.'

'Well, yes, and I was right, Miss Blake: Your adorer will now be admissible to our circle.' Caroline's eyebrows rose but she said nothing. It was Susan who said, sharply: 'Tom, do not

81

talk nonsense.'

'But it is not. We have it on your mother's authority that he may be spoken of. Though what there is to say—much less, what *he* will find to say—is problematic. Of course, Susan, you do not know the gentleman, do you? He was banished—or withdrew—before you came here.'

'No, I have never seen him,' Susan admitted. Julia laughed, falling in with Tom's mood.

'Once seen, always forgotten,' she told Susan. 'He is very dull. It is true we have seen him in town more often since Caroline was with us—'

'And he did give me fifty guineas to pay the publisher,' insisted Caroline, half ashamed now that she had shown him no gratitude. 'I did not tell you that, did I?' she added to Susan.

'It did not arise in our conversation,' Susan reassured her.

Caroline shook her head, remembering now how Mr Rushworth had flung the money at her and gone running off into the rain; he seemed gauche and pathetic. 'I hope I shall meet him again,' she sighed.

'You will have every chance I am sure,' said Tom. 'I will tell him what you say, if I meet him about the country. Sotherton is not far away. I glimpse him driving with his mother occasionally—but not on the hunting-field, needless to say—His mama dare not risk his

82

precious neck.' Tom glanced towards his own mother but she was inattentive; after divulging what thoughts she had pertaining to James Rushworth Lady Bertram had closed her eyes and drifted into a reverie on roasted apples. Tom proceeded to entertaining the others with some account of his one-time brother-in-law, of his dawdling wit and lack of humour; of his dull life in town: '—Did anyone ever hear of his throwing a party? One or two, I suppose, in Maria's day, but it was obviously she who did the throwing—And you must remember, Julia, that we launched out on some amateur theatricals, in which he was to appear in a satin cloak—'

'*Pink* satin, was it not to be?' appended Julia, amused. 'But luckily the play was never performed; he had shown that he could not memorise all his dozen lines—'

Decima giggled. 'I would have liked to see him in his costume.'

'Indeed I vow he would have made a striking figure, had he not been required to speak.'

'You see, Miss Blake,' Tom appealed to Caroline, 'what a brilliant conquest you have made.'

Caroline, intent on the work in her hands, made no acknowledgement of that; it was Susan who changed the subject, with a casual mention of the likelihood of frost tonight; and Tom aware of his own impudence allowed himself to be distracted, though his spirits remained high. Later, when the candles were brought and the gathering began to disperse for bedtime, it was Julia who was impelled to say aside:

'I feel I should apologise, Miss Blake, for the levity of my brother's manners. He does not intend to be over-familiar. It may be that he is not perfectly at ease among exclusively feminine company, but I know his only intention is to amuse and to please.'

'Perhaps it is Mr Rushworth to whom apology is due,' observed Caroline, indifferently.

If Julia took this as a reproof for her own manners, she accepted the reproof generously. 'Yes, I should not encourage Decima to make fun of the poor man,' she admitted. 'I should like to feel only that you had taken no offence.'

'I? Certainly not,' Caroline assured her with the same detachment.

What a cool little creature she is, Julia thought, as she often thought about Caroline. 'We take it, then, that he has merely been over-gallant and that you can ignore him.'

'Certainly,' said Caroline again. She saw no reason for Mrs Yates to apologise for her brother, at least where Miss Blake was concerned. It was no concern of hers, but she had perceived—and guessed—that the person whom Sir Thomas truly wished to please and amuse, and to whom his clumsy gallantries were directed, was not Miss Blake, but his

84

cousin Susan. If Mrs Yates had not guessed, it was no affair of Caroline's to point it out to her.

'Good night to you, Mrs Yates,' she said pleasantly across the candle flames.

Affairs of the heart—even that most compelling speculation: Who is in love with whom?—had had no place in Caroline's life and did not detain her now. She had a regard for Miss Price but it led towards no intimacy. This evening she had felt some compunction on hearing Mr Rushworth derided but did not suppose he would know of it, nor be troubled if he did; while Sir Thomas was of interest to her only in a negative form: She had understood that he was in no way involved in the running of the Orion theatre since Mr Stein had assumed power in it, and she had still to take some action about Stephen's verse drama: Could that ever be staged, and earn money enough to discharge the debt to her grandfather? She was settled in her mind now about Stephen's poems and their printed form, but Mr Taplow might still need persuasion; and would he—could anyone—advise her about the production of a play? If Sir Thomas chose to be facetious about Mr Rushworth, the impression made on Caroline was negligible.

Susan found Tom's heavy jocularity irritating, and was embarrassed for him, but knew Caroline to be unaffected. Tom was nowadays in a strange mood—by turns too garrulous and too sullen—but the cause of this she did not examine. Nothing of Tom's feelings had she ever related to herself.

Tom at this juncture was not at all pleased with himself. His consciousness of Susan was both puzzling and painful. When they were alone together he could not find a word to say to her; when they were in company he resented her attentions being drawn to anyone else. This middle-aged baronet felt as foolish as a schoolboy and could neither understand nor accept it. His case was perhaps similar to that of his coeval James Rushworth, but Tom had not had the training in humility to render the case sufferable. When, some days later, he chanced to encounter his long-lost brother-in-law in a Northampton street, he greeted him as warmly as if here was a chance to make amends for some offence:

'Ha—Rushworth! How d'ye do: You are staying at Sotherton, then?'

'We have been there some little while,' James told him. 'And you are at Mansfield Park?' This, from local enquiries, James knew, but he had not dared to think of any plan of approach. Nor, to his pleasure, need he:

'Lord, yes, we're all there. Why do you not visit us? Come and wait upon my mother some time. She remembers you, and company helps to make her more cheerful.'

James's face blushed with surprised delight, but as he opened his mouth to ask when such a visit might be convenient, Tom clapped him on the shoulder and strode on his way, satisfied with his own affable gesture to such an extent that he omitted to mention it at home.

Meanwhile at Mansfield Park in any case there were stirrings of departure, initiated by Julia when she received a letter from her husband reporting progress at the Orion Theatre. John Yates was diligent in writing to his wife, which was more than could be said of Mr Taplow in writing to Caroline, though it was he who had suggested their use of the postal services, and Caroline was growing anxious. This letter that Julia received made Julia both anxious and angry.

'They are to stage "The Duke's Secret" at Christmas—What nonsense,' she told Susan. 'The theatre will not possibly be ready and if they still have the properties, they will be faded and—' She flicked over the page, adding: '—And it is a worthless little *Singspiel* that no one will—No, this I will *not* have!' she cried, reading aloud: '"I have promised Mortimer the role of the blackamoor servant-boy." Promised? I will put a stop to that. I will not have that boy taken out of school when he is settling there—I must go back to town at once,' she exclaimed with fervour.

'And I will come with you Mama,' Decima hastened to say; she was eager to see how the new theatre did, and welcomed a change of society from that of her prim Parsonage cousins.

'Very well. You need new clothes. And Tom can take us.'

'I?' said Tom uncertainly.

'Yes, you. You have been talking about giving up the lease of your town house but have done nothing about it. And you have done nothing here but go hunting and amuse yourself.'

'And surely,' Decima urged him, 'you want to see how the Orion is looking and how the rehearsals go?'

Tom had indeed been tempted. He glanced at Susan who did not raise her eyes from the book she had been reading to Lady Bertram. 'I do not wish to leave our mother alone—' he began.

'She will have Susan. She always has Susan,' said Julia impatiently. 'And, Miss Blake, you will come with us? I know you feel you should visit your publisher-man.'

'I would be very grateful—'

'Then let it be arranged. We shall all go to our house while you and Tom see to your own business and I see to Mortimer. And his father. Do you hear us, ma'am?' she addressed Lady Bertram. 'We are going to town, but not for long. We shall be back for Mortimer's Christmas holidays, all together, and make it a happy time for you. Will you like that?'

'Just as you please, my dear,' said her mother. 'Go on, Susan; was that the end of the chapter?'

'Almost,' said Susan who had kept her finger on the page. Tom failed to catch her eye and had no idea how she felt at the plan of this general departure; it occurred to him that no one could ever guess what Susan was thinking.

CHAPTER TEN

It came about, then, that by the time James Rushworth could act upon his invitation to Mansfield Park, only Lady Bertram and Miss Price were there to receive him.

The invitation, at that accidental meeting with Tom Bertram, had been a great stroke of luck. James had been ranging about the countryside in the hope of such an encounter, sometimes to the puzzlement of his mother:

'Why need you go *looking* for the stonemason, James—Why not simply send for him?'

But James would go about things in his own way, and since he was attending carefully to his estate duties, she should have no complaint. This, naturally, worried her; but he appeared happy enough; he strolled about, whistling like a ploughboy, always busy in his plodding fashion; she had no cause for worry, and in this state she was at a loss; there must be something to worry about; and this brought her son a second stroke of luck: Her mind turned to her own health, to her rheumatic symptoms and the useless physicians she had consulted in London; and to the worries about her house in Bath, left to the unreliable servants at this time of year, with winter upon them. She had meant to be away for only a short time and had been distracted by the necessity of rescuing James from the vicious life of London. Well, and had that not been achieved? She could never achieve peace of mind about her son but he seemed contented and peaceful-minded himself and she decided to take the risk of leaving him at Sotherton alone, for the present.

James dutifully escorted his mother to Bath but would remain there for only a couple of nights. He set off back to Sotherton leaving her in another of her constant perplexities: She knew that James did not care for Bath; but where else in the kingdom could one find young ladies suitable for him? Mrs Rushworth had not yet lost the hope of his re-marrying, suitably, and providing that heir to Sotherton.

She worried about this but when she made the suggestion to James he would say: 'Well, but I did marry, did I not, and a fine disaster I made of it.'

'I do not wonder, with the flighty girl you chose. Not all women are of her sort, you know.'

James supposed that they were not, but he

did not attempt to explain his thoughts—insofar as he himself understood them—to his mother. The charm of Miss Blake, his Ondine, lay in her remoteness; she was to be adored from a quality of distance that held none of the threats he recollected in the domestic struggles of marriage. He felt so little claim on her that he was not much distressed when he made his way to Mansfield Park to discover that she was gone to London. Almost it was a relief not to confront her, but to be received by Lady Bertram and Miss Price, with civility and justifiable surprise, which was quickly dispelled when he explained that Tom had asked him to call.

'It is good of you to come,' Miss Price assured him. 'You have ridden over from Sotherton? I hope the roads are not icy.'

Surprised Susan was, but she was also interested to meet this family joke in person and to find him personable enough. It was not that she would have expected him to arrive in a pink satin cloak and to mutter like an idiot or to sit in a witless silence; indeed, he expressed his condolences to Lady Bertram on the loss of her husband, belated as they were, with the formality of a rehearsed speech and with some composure.

'I visited Sotherton once,' announced Lady Bertram, with pride. 'I remember. It is a large and handsome house.'

'Indeed, ma'am, I hope you will come again.

And . . . Miss Price too.' He added doubtfully: '. . . And all the members of your family,' not yet understanding whether Miss Price counted among those.

'Just now they are all gone up to town,' Lady Bertram told him. 'But they are all coming again at Christmas, they tell me, bringing that noisy little boy Mortimer, and Miss Blake. There is so much coming and going, but I do not mind it. It keeps me from dwelling on my sorrow.'

Susan, noticing the change in Mr Rushworth's face at the mention of Miss Blake's name, was enlightened as to the probable motive for his visit. She said: 'We are happy to have Miss Blake here. She and I have become good friends,' and was rewarded by a beaming smile from the visitor, who turned towards her, the smile succeeded by a puckered brow as he asked eagerly:

'She—Miss Blake—I am glad she has such good friends—But has she no family—no people of her own?'

Susan considered this. 'Do you know—it seems strange, but I have to admit we know very little about her. We hear only that she had a brother who died. The poet, you know?—Of course you do. Where his work is concerned you have been the best of Miss Blake's friends, already. I think she cares more for her brother's writings than for anything else in the world.'

This for some reason appeared to please him. He shrugged off the hint about his generosity to Miss Blake, and half-smiling, nodded to himself. It pleased him that Miss Blake should exist chiefly in an other-worldly element, unattached. He thought: She is a poem herself.

'What a beautiful thing to say!' exclaimed Miss Price.

Horrified, he gazed at Miss Price with an expression that might have excused anyone for thinking him moronic. He had *said* it? He had an idea that he did utter his thoughts aloud sometimes, in the freedom of his new secret life; it was on a par with the whistling that so annoyed his mother; but now—How could he make such a crazy fool of himself—like this— before a stranger? He coughed, shuffled his feet, and glanced in appeal towards Lady Bertram—who had evidently fallen asleep, leaving him alone with this radiant Miss Price and her perceptiveness—which he could not avoid; she had been sincere; for the first time in his life being credited with saying a beautiful thing, James would almost rather she had laughed at him or scorned him.

Susan for her part was delighted by his utterance. She could recognise romantic worship, perhaps remembering the feeling she had denied her cousin Tom as a young girl; to recognise it in a man who must be all of forty years of age did not rouse her derision; she was touched and respectful. However, she had to respect his dignity, and sympathised with his painful embarrassment; she must turn the conversation in a more normal direction.

'You are fond of poetry yourself?' she suggested.

'Yes—That is, no. I cannot make sense of it as a rule.' He could not dissemble, or care what Miss Price might think of him. He longed only to be gone, and Susan needed not to be perceptive to guess that. She must let him go. She woke Lady Bertram to set the farewells in train, and he civilly took his leave, with no response to the hopes of either lady that he would call again.

'I should have asked him how his mother did,' Lady Bertram recalled. 'Is she still alive? She was a rather vulgar little woman, as I remember. She had no fortune and was too proud of her wealthy house. But her son is a pleasant polite boy. I do not know why Tom and Julia think he is comical.'

'Nor do I, ma'am,' replied Susan.

She was left wondering whether Mr Rushworth would visit Mansfield Park while Caroline was here at Christmas; and, for that matter, about Caroline herself: had she any other relatives or friends in the world, and what could she do when her brother's poems were finally published and her life's work, as she saw it, accomplished? Even a living 'poem' must be fed and supported and perhaps work for its keep. Well, Caroline was a fine needlewoman and had, from what she said, supported her brother and herself thereby at some time. Susan had leisure enough just now to wonder about everyone else's future; her own was bounded again by Lady Bertram's embroidery; Mr Rushworth's visit had provided the agreeable sight of a new face in a house more quiet than, it seemed to Susan, it had ever been.

The house in Marylebone was, by contrast, in turmoil. Tom did earnestly mean to set about the arrangements for relinquishing his own house, but he found that this would involve more lawyers, as well as inventories, surveys, and the disposal of many of his possessions which must be despatched to Mansfield; from all this he was soon distracted by the state of matters at the Orion Theatre. It was obvious that 'The Duke's Secret' was in no way to be staged by Christmas, if at all; John Yates and his new partner Stein had it all in a muddle; Master Mortimer had taken his omission hard, and his mother and father were at loggerheads about him, and about Decima, who was more stagestruck than anyone; Stein had secured Hilde Buchspiel again as the Duchess, who now wanted the whole libretto translated from Italian into German; in all, a fresh mind and a little organising power was needed—Tom was needed—but no one was at all grateful for his advice. He could now barely remember how it was that he had come to be ousted from his part in the enterprise, and his exclusion did not improve his temper.

Julia remarked to her husband: 'I do not know who invited Tom to take up residence in our house. Let us hope that he will soon give his mind to his own affairs and relieve us of his presence—'

'I do not know,' said John Yates, 'why he cannot stay at his club, for instance, if he must leave his house free. I have enough on my mind without *Sir* Thomas storming in and out—'

This followed an announcement of Tom's that he would need the carriage on the following day to visit his solicitors. Julia had inquired whether a cab might not be as suitable? Upon which, Tom had left the room slamming the door. Decima, who was at the table with Caroline, cast her eyes heavenward; but Caroline took the opportunity of saying what had been on her mind:

'Mrs Yates—I too, you know, have come uninvited into your house and should soon seek some permanent dwelling and way of life—'

Her hearers laughed. 'My dear Caroline,' cried Julia, 'we none of us supposed you needed invitation. For myself, I am comforted to have one member of the household who is not in a ferment over something.'

'Mrs Rigg gave me my pin-money again,

when we came back from Mansfield,' Caroline mentioned. 'But that is—'

'That is not enough, and I see you are working at Mortimer's shirt ruffles,' said Julia, feeling that the family owed Caroline—what? Gratitude and some compassion? Decima said:

'You must not leave us. Where might you go?'

'I did not mean that I deserve more than my pin-money,' said Caroline to Julia. 'Your kindness to me has been more than I can say. You have made it possible for me to await Mr Taplow's work on the book in the company of friends—'

'We, and Mr Rushworth,' put in Decima in a teasing tone; Caroline ignoring her went on:

'It may be that when I have seen him tomorrow I shall be able to make some decisions—though I do not know—'

'He is being horribly slow,' Decima sighed. 'Does he truly mean to publish the book?'

Caroline winced a little at this ruthless question, but John Yates interrupted, folding his newspaper:

'If Tom is to have the carriage he can take Miss Blake to her publisher and bring her home. It is the least he can do, and this is no weather for her to be out.' Wintry rain was darkening the windows. Tom, told of this plan, supposed that he might convey Miss Blake as long as it did not take him too far out of his way; he must be at the Orion by noon to sort out some problem concerning the stage lamps. He felt that Julia and John conspired to put difficulties in his way; it was tiresome of Julia to be so inconsiderate of her own brother when he was virtually homeless. Caroline, nervous of meeting the tardy Mr Taplow face to face, was equally nervous of Tom's temper and misdirected him twice through the sodden streets; when he left her, his curt: 'I shall call for you in a half hour—' sounded like a threat.

Since his solicitors did not long detain him, his temper had improved when, five and twenty minutes later, he returned to the publisher's premises, though his purpose was sharpened. Impatient of the clatter of rain on the carriage roof he not only sent the servant to announce that Sir Thomas Bertram had called for Miss Blake, but followed the man indoors to emphasize his point, pursuing the clerk through a mean little vestibule into a back room where Miss Blake was in conference with a scraggy young man in eyeglasses.

'You are ready, Miss Blake?'

The little man took it upon himself to reply: 'We are ready, I think, sir—There was one small matter, Miss Blake'—at which Tom sighed loudly—'Just, about complimentary copies; I will send them to the usual critics—though I am afraid we may not expect much notice—Can you suggest any recipients?'

Caroline, not altogether sure what he

meant, recollected: 'I did want to send a copy to Mr Piper—Stephen's schoolmaster—'

'Yes, yes . . . If you would give me his address—' As she wrote this out Tom demanded:

'So the famous poetry is to appear at last?'

'Yes, yes—Except that this is not a good time of year—So close to Christmas—'

'I cannot see why not,' Tom observed in an implacable tone. 'As from what I am told, this is to be a small edition, I imagine you could have had it printed, bound and covered within a week.' His glance round the room had a scathing quality as if he now saw how unlikely that was in such surroundings.

Mr Taplow began to feel that he could and should carry out the plan. He was not used to having baronets burst into his office and doubt his efficiency: he had left Miss Blake's work aside, being ambitious for more lucrative enterprises. He murmured:

'If you wish it, I will have it done at once. Indeed, yes. I will set everything else aside. Miss Blake and I,' he added, pushing up his eyeglasses, 'were also discussing the possibilities of another work of her brother's— his verse drama—'

'Drama.' The baronet tossed the word away. 'I do not suppose that will concern you. Miss Blake has friends who own a theatre.' He laid his hand on the back of Caroline's chair as if to tip her off it. 'Now, if you will excuse us—I have an appointment.'

When they had left Mr Taplow removed his eyeglasses and rubbed his eyes, marvelling at Miss Blake, so modest and obstinate, who could summon wealthy, titled and even theatrical champions. It caused him to value her brother's poetry more highly. She should have her little book immediately—that is, as soon as it could be managed. He would send for his foreman printer this very morning.

Caroline and Tom ran through the rain to the carriage. As he handed her in he saw that she was laughing.

'Sir Thomas—I believe you frightened him!'

'I hope so. It is time that someone did,' said Tom, not displeased with himself.

'I admit,' went on Caroline more seriously, 'that what you told him about Stephen's verse drama was ... part of the frightening. I know—and what I have seen of the activity at the Orion shows me—that there is a great deal more to the staging of a play than I had imagined, or could expect anyone to undertake.'

'Yes, well, what goes on at the Orion is pandemonium,' said Tom, scornfully, his thoughts now running ahead. 'They are a set of hopeless amateurs.' He would, however, be there in good time after all; he had dealt with the solicitors and with Mr Taplow in peremptory style and had the rest of the day before him. 'Oh, while I remember; if Decima is at the Orion, her mother wants you to take her home.'

'If she will come—'

'She will, if I tell her to,' decided Decima's uncle.

She probably would, but under protest. Caroline found her duties as chaperone a little unhappy at present. Decima was living in a drama of her own: She was suffering unrequited love for a certain Arturo Lasso, a tenor who had joined the cast of 'The Duke's Secret' in the role of the Duke's profligate (and hence secret) brother. Decima's passion too was a secret, of which her family was fully aware as she languished and suffered, but no one spoke of it or took it too seriously as long as Decima avoided indiscretion. Julia respected her daughter's 'ferment' and tried to keep her away from rehearsals on any pretext; Signor Lasso had no idea of it, and perhaps even Decima would have thought it better so; but as she came out of the theatre and joined Caroline in the carriage she complained:

'I do not know why Mama sends for me in *case* the bootmaker comes. I am sure he is not due until Thursday. She treats me like a child. I have no life of my own . . .'

'You will be "out" soon after Christmas, and then—'

'That does not console me. Oh, Caroline, I am so unhappy. You are my only faithful friend, because you do not ask *questions* and want to discover my private feelings . . .'

Of course Decima would have enjoyed nothing more than to describe her private feelings, but she did not expect to arouse any curiosity in Caroline and was not sorry for that. She said, deeply confidential: 'I *could* talk to you I think. But to no one else. Why is it, that *old* people do not understand love?'

'It may be that they have forgotten—'

'I meant, people like my Uncle Tom. I do not suppose he was ever in love in his life.'

'Nor was I,' admitted Caroline, looking back and wondering why not.

Decima gave a tragic sigh and murmured: 'Oh, you are *lucky*.'

CHAPTER ELEVEN

While London was in gloom and sooty rain, Northamptonshire was mild and fair, which pleased Susan because she was able to go out of doors. Tom liked her, when she could be spared for an hour or so, to exercise a little roan mare he called his 'lady's horse'. She enjoyed the exercise herself, and one morning when she was already mounted, and James Rushworth rode into the stable yard with the intention of calling on Lady Bertram, she instantly invited him to accompany her on her circuit of the park, and he as instantly changed his plans; and so they rode out together.

'We—Lady Bertram and I—are still alone here,' Susan said. 'But as far as we are told, we shall have everyone back for Christmas. Will you be at Sotherton then?'

'My mother wishes me to join her in Bath,' said James in a tone of no great pleasure. 'I shall be sorry not to see—everyone.'

They approached a gateway; with his whip, James flicked up the latch and swung open the gate for Susan to ride through. She noticed how deft he was with his strong-looking hands; she was disposed to look for virtues in Mr Rushworth, as if to compensate for her family's denigration of him. She suspected that he longed to speak of Caroline yet was loth to introduce the topic. Today, though, there was an item that could reasonably interest him:

'I believe that the book of poems is more likely to appear at last. That is because Tom went to see the publisher and spoke up for her—or so he claims.'

'He writes to tell you this?' asked Mr Rushworth, resentful—that anyone else should do for Caroline more than he could.

'*Tom* write letters?' cried Susan, ironically. 'No indeed. It was Caroline who wrote to tell me. Anyway Tom is too busy, doing everything at once and achieving nothing, I gather; I hope his mood has improved by the time he comes home. I expect it will; he has all manner of amusements in town, but he is a countryman at heart.'

James observed to himself: She speaks a deal about her cousin Tom. It could be that they are very fond of each other. He did not ponder this, for just then as they turned on to a long rising grass track, Miss Price said: 'I usually let Demoiselle have a canter here, up to the Lodge gates—' and before James could more than deduce that 'Demoiselle' was the name of her horse, she had increased her pace and drawn swiftly ahead. James's own horse, as surprised as he, made a vigorous bound to catch up, and before he could rein back Miss Price called over her shoulder: '—A race, then?' and off she sped, the mare skimming the ground, while James felt his steed gathering strength as if refusing to be outrun by a mere female of his species. James's instinct had been to keep close to Miss Price lest her speed bring her into danger, but the mare was light as a cat and the pounding hooves of her rival brought him to the Lodge gates the winner by only half a head, horse and James both almost breathless.

'Well ridden, ma'am!' James acclaimed her.

'Thank you, sir—That was most enjoyable. Now I should have Demoiselle walk until she is cool; Tom would not like to see her lathered like this; it was an unseemly gallop.'

Tom again. Well, but his little horse had enjoyed it too; and James could admit that he too had been included in the excitement; he

104

was aware of a deep respect and an easy friendliness towards Miss Price, who had guessed and guarded his secret, and was moreover an excellent horsewoman. The party proceeded decorously back to the stables, where Tom's head stableman, a stern Yorkshireman named Culthorpe, was ready to run a critical hand down Demoiselle's legs before Miss Price had even dismounted. His nod of approval was to James's relief, but as he set off homewards he recognised that there might not be any more happy mornings like this; Christmas was almost upon them, and wintry weather could not be far behind. And interveningly, the dankness and artificial socialising of Bath. And would he see Miss Blake, at all?

He prepared for his sojourn in Bath with no expectation of gaiety, and it must be confessed that not all the guests at Mansfield Park arrived in cheerful spirits. John Yates was despondent about 'The Duke's Secret', whose rehearsals had been 'suspended' (until who knew when?) and the cast dispersed; Signor Lasso had retreated with his wife and five children to a rented house in Hampstead, leaving Decima bereft; young Mortimer who had looked forward to parties with his schoolfriends in town considered himself banished to rustic boredom; Julia was afraid that family disunity would be only the worse for another rural episode. Lady Bertram was descending into a trough of sadness as the memories of happier old Yuletides assailed her; Tom was altogether dejected in his failure to solve any of his problems or to find any amusement in his inescapably dutiful life.

One comfort he would have: He would be with Susan again and could be sure of her help and sympathy. That alone would cheer him up. Susan would listen to him and tell him what to do. He had never before valued her as highly or felt such need of her, and as he brooded upon this he came to perceive whither it led him and to wonder why it had not been so clear to him long ago.

Among them all, Caroline was now amazingly happy, but conscious of the general malaise she did not say so. Mr Taplow, just two days before the departure for Mansfield Park, had sent his clerk to her with a parcel containing six copies of POEMS OF STEPHEN BLAKE for her own use. She had not expected this—or to see the poems in print at all; it must fairly be admitted that Mr Taplow had completed his task with commendable speed and admirable taste. The little book, covered in dark green, its title in gold letters, and free of the editor's changes that had so much distressed her, seemed as she held it in her hands to speak for Stephen; the voice of his imagination sounded from the pages, simple and sweet as if he spoke to her. She could not have believed that the mere printed letters, after her own handwriting, could bring about such a transformation. Indeed she had almost lost hope of the outcome and it rose phoenix-like from that despair—more wonderful than any belief.

She showed the books to Susan, who was sincerely appreciative of the poems. 'It was worth all your worry and trouble,' she told Caroline. 'The language appears simple but I can see it is cleverly crafted—And how it makes me see the wild moorland landscape, though I have never been further north than Northamptonshire. Your brother must have loved it—I do not wonder that you loved *him*!'

This was highly gratifying. 'I would like you to have a copy, to keep,' Caroline told her. 'I wanted to ask you: Should I give a copy to Mr Rushworth too? It was he who made it all possible.'

'He would be pleased with the gesture but I am not sure that he would read the poems,' said Susan with candour. 'Would that not be a waste?'

'For that matter, it was Sir Thomas who frightened Mr Taplow into action finally,' Caroline added.

'Oh, do call him Tom!' said Susan with a touch of impatience.

'I do, sometimes, when I forget. He is not quite what I imagined a baronet to be. Nor is that uncomplimentary—'

Susan could have agreed but did not pursue

the matter. It had seemed to her that Tom since he had arrived on this visit had been behaving oddly; like or unlike a baronet, he had been either more offhand than was normal in him, or more loquacious; he did not listen to what she said to him, or replied at random out of some inner preoccupation. He might have been a man with something on his mind; but if something there were, it was unusual that he could not communicate it to Susan, his confidante among the family. Susan supposed that she would in time be enlightened and did not inquire. Perhaps they were all a little depressed by the atmosphere of this unfestive Christmas. Even the weather had darkened. On Christmas Day when Lady Bertram attended church heavily veiled, with the coachman in mourning ribbons, the occasion inevitably suggested the funereal. Later on that day, when Lady Bertram had had a little sleep and a little mulled wine, she was able to join in the general conversation round the fireside, in which Julia encouraged her.

'. . . And you have not been too lonely ma'am, while we were all back in town?'

'Oh no. I always have Susan.'

'And you have been receiving visitors?'

'Oh yes, Dr Stevenson called. And Mr Rushworth.'

'Rushworth?' exclaimed Tom. 'What could *he* want?'

At the mention of the name Julia had

looked up smiling, while an audible titter sounded from Decima's side of the hearth. Susan said:

'Mr Rushworth told us that you had invited him to call, Tom.'

'Well if I did—'

'He was very polite,' remarked Lady Bertram. 'And he went out riding with Susan.'

Tom's glance, to which Susan did not raise her head, was almost a glare; she said calmly:

'I have had Demoiselle round the park more than twice a week while the weather has been so mild.'

'With Rushworth?'

'Once. I am sorry that you must have missed some good hunting.'

Tom shrugged as if indifferent to that. Indeed he was totally indifferent to James Rushworth, and was annoyed with himself for letting it seem that he suffered anything so trivial as jealousy. In general he was at present troubled by strange anxieties and fears—he saw Susan too as strange, more lovely and graceful than he had ever observed; could it be his dear friend Susan whom he dared not—yet must—approach? And on such strange new terms?

Susan too was aware of a difference in him that she could not explain, but she did not require him to either. He appeared now and then to be on the point of saying something that was checked by an embarrassment unusual in him; but when, two days after Christmas, the two of them were alone in the office room that they had shared since the death of Sir Thomas and Tom accidentally revealed his feelings, she was taken by surprise.

Tom was speaking of the complications involved in the giving up of his London house and added: 'It is all so tiresome, but it must be done, I know—it is a mere extravagance—besides, you do not care for London, do you? We should have no *need* of a house there.'

'*I?*' cried Susan. 'How do I come into the matter?'

'Oh, you must know what I mean—I did not mean to say—That is, I have been meaning to for so long—Susan, you must have guessed what has been so much on my mind—' he floundered, then committed himself in a tone of command rather than of persuasion: 'I want you to marry me!'

Susan received this with a broad smile and a little sigh of what sounded like relief; she could not more clearly have said: 'Is *that* all!' Surprised she was, but in no way discomfited. 'Oh, no, Tom, that would not do at all.'

'But why *not*?' he inevitably demanded. He had thought of no objections and was slow to summon them now: Cousins marrying? There was already a perfectly happy example of that in the family. Money? Susan had no fortune but he and she would not care about that. She would not need to leave Mansfield Park or desert Lady Bertram; Susan must be glad to think of herself as the next Lady Bertram; heirs to Mansfield? There were nephews at the Parsonage, should Susan not wish for children of her own. It all seemed to Tom so practical and obvious. And if he had Susan always by him, he could settle as a country squire and she would support and help him in all the duties of that.

Susan would have agreed with him on all these points but the insuperable drawback was that she did not love him. Indeed, all the duties and pleasures of her life here she already enjoyed. Tom as a husband she had never conceived of, and she did not imagine that he would be happy with her in that relationship. Nor did he love her. She did not invite any protestations that this statement might bring upon her, but shook her head in gentle denial.

She had been immunised against love for him before any possibility of love had even arisen; she had forgotten making that negative decision but she must stand by it, because on it rested all the affectionate friendship that had grown and lasted between the two of them for so many years. It was precious to her and she knew quite well that she had occupied a place in Tom's own life that was unique and valuable to him. Even now, when he had spoken out, something had changed; Tom liked his own way; he would not be dissuaded. He must have Susan for his own—Why? Because he was sure of her and 'playing safe'? She sighed again, this time wearily. She was afraid a battle might lie ahead for which she might possess the courage but not the spirit.

'You have not heard the last of this,' Tom muttered, leaning back against the window sill as if weary himself. 'I shall leave the Orion Theatre to ruin itself, and stay here at Mansfield until you yield.'

If he were to quit his theatrical adventures, Susan reflected, that might be to his advantage. She wished he did not look so sad, drooping against the grey winter light of the window. 'I shall be glad if you stay here,' she told him without enthusiasm. But it would not be the same.

It had never occurred to Susan that she herself held a positive place in Tom's private life—that she could ever affect or hurt him. Now he made her feel cruel and heartless—the anguish of it struck her painfully but she could not 'yield'.

'One thing I am going to do,' Tom said a little more briskly, levering himself up from the sill, 'is to give you Demoiselle for your own, and tell my mother that you are to ride out as often as you wish. Let Decima thread her needles, or whatever it is she requires.'

Susan tried to say; 'Thank you . . .' but her voice was husky. Nor did Tom wait for thanks. As he passed her on the way to the door she noticed that his face was stiff and darkened . . .

Older? In some way, it was suddenly more like the face of a baronet.

CHAPTER TWELVE

Tom's proposal to Susan was not concealed from the household; Susan herself felt obliged to inform Lady Bertram of it; nor was she afraid of everyone's advice—which was entirely in favour of its acceptance. Lady Bertram said: 'Now I shall not have to manage without you!' and John Yates was heard to declare to his wife: 'I do not know why Tom did not think of it years ago!' In fact, no one took her refusal of Tom at all seriously. Susan felt it disloyal to Tom to elaborate on her own motives; and it was borne on the family only by his sombre remoteness that Tom was disappointed and serious enough about that. His wretchedness began gradually to pervade the house as the new year began in chill and fog.

Julia with sisterly frankness said: 'Susan, I do wish you would change your mind and accept the poor man. You are the only one who can keep him in order!' Young Mortimer remarked to his sister: 'I should think Susan cannot expect any more chances at her age?' Decima despising such base reasoning—for her, passion must always be tragic, and she was

113

consigned herself to unrequited love—said: 'How little you understand at *your* age. Marriage is not everything.' She was pursuing a feud with her father and mother: She would not undertake, on returning to town, to avoid the Orion in whatever plight it might be, or to eschew the society of Signor Lasso (to whom, it need not be mentioned, she had spoken a bare few words in her life.) It was, announced Decima, a matter of principle: she did not care if the modest 'coming out' party planned for her did not take place; she saw it as punishment bravely borne if she therefore had to stay at Mansfield while her family returned, her father to his theatre and Mortimer to school. Punishment this was intended to be, but Decima would not weaken. Also she considered that Susan was perfectly right not to marry Tom if she did not want to. 'It would all just be too *tidy*,' she opined, 'making everybody happy and leaving everything just the same.' That was not how life should be arranged for the truly romantic. Susan had never seemed to Decima to be a romantic character—she was so *good* and sensible and cheerful—besides being on the verge of middle age—but Decima had to admire someone who rejected the baronet and his estate in favour of acting as lady-in-waiting to her grandmother, and so far had been cheerful about that.

So far . . . But in the reduced household, as days passed, Susan began to sense an emptiness that she had not hitherto. She and Tom did not avoid one another; there were still the affairs of Sir Thomas's will to be dealt with; local affairs multiplied; as usual Tom and Susan worked in the office room; Tom made an evident effort to keep up with matters, but drove himself into fits of impatience, especially when the weather cleared again and he felt imprisoned. More, it struck him for the first time that Susan spent too much of her time with ledgers and desk. 'I do not understand,' he burst out one day, 'how you came to commit yourself to these labours. What was my father about, to let you toil as secretary to him—'

Firstly, Sir Thomas had been fond of Susan and glad to have her company and help; and secondly, Sir Thomas's son and heir had been so often in town or on the hunting field that he was rarely *au fait* with what went on in the office. Susan not long ago would have said so, perhaps forcibly, but now she had no suggestions to offer.

One morning when the post was due, and she had settled Lady Bertram to stitching pink rosebuds along a runner, Susan went into the office to find Draper sitting at her desk. This gentleman's official title was 'librarian'; he had been secretary to Sir Thomas until his eyesight began to fail and his spelling errors to proliferate, while Sir Thomas had been in rather similar case. Now Draper beamed upon Susan:

115

'Good morning, Miss Price. Sir Thomas has decided that I may help him in the office for two hours each morning, to set you free to go riding or what you will. I am so pleased to feel that I am of some use again and I am sure you are grateful to him.'

Draper was so clearly pleased that Susan beamed back at him before returning to the drawingroom, where Caroline had arrived and was disentangling skeins of silk. Lady Bertram was pleased as well to hear of Draper's reappearance.

'How thoughtful of Tom. It shows how highly he regards you, does it not, Susan?— No, you must go and amuse yourself; Tom would want you to feel perfectly free. Caroline and I are managing nicely.'

What Susan was tempted to feel was perfectly unwanted. She beamed at this pair, and withdrew, perverse only in deciding that she would not ride out on Demoiselle in case Tom were watching from a window. Instead she went to her room and wrote letters to her mother and her eldest brother William the Rear Admiral; to the latter she had always written when in need of comfort, but indeed there had been no 'always' about it; she had had no complaints of Mansfield Park.

This was pointed out to her later when she walked down to the Parsonage. 'But even if you decide not to marry Tom,' her elder sister persuaded her, 'you must not feel displaced

116

there. They have all been so kind to you and can not wish to lose you. And I am sure that this Miss Blake—Caroline?—does not wish to displace you at all. You have much to be grateful for.'

Susan had been grateful to Caroline recently for her disinclination to discuss the situation of Tom at all; Caroline dreaming over her poetry book was safe from the subtle unrest of the household. Nor was she offering more than passing help to Lady Bertram; no more than Decima did she enjoy unravelling tangled silks. As for the advent of Draper, that problem would solve itself in a way that Susan, knowing Tom, foresaw. It was only a couple of days later that when Draper had completed his two hours and left Tom groaned:

'This old dotard is impossible. Will you *look* at this letter he took at my dictation—I cannot send it—'

Susan, who had come quietly into the office in search of ink, looked at it. 'But he is so pleased to be useful—'

'*Pah.*'

'How would it be,' said Susan glancing at the shelves, 'if we asked him to make a new copy of that "Repairs and Materials" ledger that is so old it is dropping to pieces? He could sit in the corner by the window where the light is best, and it would keep him busy—'

'—And it would not matter if he spelt every word wrong,' said Tom, smiling. 'I knew you

117

would think of something.' That, and his smile, set them again on their old terms for a moment. So Mr Draper took up his new task, and Susan resumed her desk, and she and Tom were on their normal footing while a third person was present; they could speak more naturally with Draper scratching and blinking away in his corner. But it was not the same, and never would be again.

Decima, flagging a little in her self-immolation, asked whether she might ride Demoiselle in the park occasionally? Susan did not know how Tom might take that; it was strange to her, not to be able to judge Tom's reactions. He had had a few days' hunting but had not offered to ride out with Susan as he had been used to. Not wanting to deny Decima, Susan approached him:

'Do you think Decima is a good rider? She wants to borrow Demoiselle but should I allow her to—'

'It is your own horse, my dear,' said Tom wih utter indifference.

It was at this moment that Susan admitted a decision that had been working its way to the surface of her mind against her will: I shall have to go away. I shall have to leave Mansfied altogether.

Where she might go, was of secondary importance as she gazed across a great fissure that had opened in her life; she was horrified but resolute; her position here, in the true home of her life, had become untenable. Tom, if he did not see that, had nevertheless seen to it. She was an obstacle to his happiness and he himself could do nothing to remove it except in her absence. She was convinced that he did need and want a wife: that he had, as it were, taken the nearest; but that he must have a clean new heart to offer, to feel true love.

The question of where Susan should go, or what she should do, was the chief preoccupation of everyone who heard of her leaving. Lady Bertram refused to believe her at all. 'Oh no, Susan dear, you cannot go away. We cannot spare you. Let us hear no more about it.' Julia, to whom Lady Bertram must have written, wrote affectionately: '. . . I can believe that you do not care to take on Tom as a husband but feel you were our last hope. But what will you do? Must you seek a position of governess or schoolteacher or some such terrible fate? We have all treated you rather as a poor relation and made use of you in a way I am ashamed of. You must have a free life of your own at last. If you need a little time to seek a course of action, you must stay here with us, and I will forbid Tom the house while you are in it . . .'

At least Julia was aware of Susan's plight, though she could suggest no solution. Susan was also fortified by a letter from Rear Admiral William Price, RN, in answer to hers:

'. . . I read between the lines, as the saying goes, that you felt in very low spirits when you wrote to me. In fact you were for some reason thinking of leaving Mansfield Park and its beloved kindly inhabitants. It is high time. What I must warn you of is that all goes on as usual near Portsmouth. Sam's wife has run away from him and arrived with two children and a dog. Betsy expects her lying-in in a couple of weeks and her husband is in Malta. The house has become infested with fleas—from the dog? The servant has stolen the silver spoons and vanished. Mama owes the butcher sixteen pounds and has a headache because she cannot find her reading glasses. She is at her wits' end and begs you to come to her assistance. My earnest advice to you is: DO NOT COME. You would be *beyond* your own wits' end after one week. I promise you we are all doing our best for her as always but we wish to spare you. I am to be in Gibraltar next month but will write to you if it would be redirected from Mansfield?

YOUR AFFEC. BRO.,
WILLIAM.'

Marylebone, and now Portsmouth, provided two solid if unprofitable points on earth to which Susan could refer; the world beyond Mansfield acquired a little reality. Presently Tom, who on first hearing of her intended departure had said merely: 'Nonsense!' now produced a suggestion:

'Why do you talk of going away?' he grumbled, approaching Susan on the terrace where she was trying to stir the fat little pugs to take exercise. 'Where do you want to *go*?'

'You told me yourself, not so long ago, that I ought to see more of the world.'

'Did I? Well, and *you* told *me* I must marry.'

'So you must. But not—'

'I will tell you what we will do,' interrupted Tom, prodding with his foot at the fattest pug, and smiling all at once. 'We shall marry soon— before Lent—and then sail away to the Indies. Would not that be a splendid wedding journey? I know I must visit those plantations and decide what is to be done with them. So we shall sail the ocean together and see Antigua—That surely is the world, for you?'

Surely it was; but Susan recognised that it was a dream of escape and adventure that attracted him; he was still half schoolboy as well as half baronet. She repeated to herself: I must go away. She smiled and shook her head, denying his whim but hating to deprive him of it.

Reminding herself constantly that she must go away, she could not help lingering; time hung, there was no initiative. She could not pack her box and depart like a dismissed housemaid; nor did anyone want her to leave—indeed she hated the idea herself. She was not destitute; her uncle had willed her a legacy adequate to her subsistence. She sent her mother some money, for the butcher and for new eyeglasses, and set herself as if to wait out the winter evenings that Lady Bertram had so passionately dreaded. The life of the house proceeded equably; everyone might have been waiting for a decision from Susan but it was not discussed. A kind of polite non-expectation prevailed. After tea Tom and the three young ladies might play a hand of whist, or Decima play the pianoforte, or Susan read aloud. When Lady Bertram's maid came to see her to bed, the others might stay on at the fireside in casual chat. Tom had an air of absent-mindedness but seemed prepared to make himself agreeable. One evening, when Lady Bertram had asked him to undertake the reading, choosing speeches from Shakespeare's *As You Like It*, Caroline listened intently and said afterwards:

'How well you read! It is no wonder that you are interested in the theatre.'

'That may derive from my practice in this very room during school holidays,' he said, amused. 'My brother and I had to render "The quality of mercy"—or "My name is Norval" often enough, to our father's exacting standards.' He added, to please her, some question about her brother's verse drama; had she a copy he might look at? Caroline leapt up very readily and ran to find it. Susan approved his kindness, privately dreading at times the descent to earth that might overtake Caroline when the euphoria over Stephen's poems subsided; Caroline had still her difficulties and was almost as undecided over her course of life as Susan herself. Tom, flicking over the pages of the large notebook, said:

'M'm; this is about the death of Socrates, I see; can there be enough action in it, for a stage play? Is not your hero flat on his back quaffing hemlock?'

'Oh no—You will see; there are scenes from his earlier life, and Stephen brings Xantippe into it—'

'—Which is more than Socrates did,' murmured Tom, reading. 'Is this your only copy?' he asked.

'Yes, this is Stephen's original. I cannot part with it. I left my own copy with Mr Taplow.'

'*Pah*. It will go no further there. What you should do, you know, with a new drama like this, is to try it on an actor, not a fussy backstreet publisher.'

'An actor?' echoed Caroline, not in the least offended, Susan was glad to observe, by the teasing quality of Tom's remarks.

'Yes; if you can interest a well-known actor in a part, he will see to it that the play is staged. Take a man who fancies himself as a great tragedian—who can choose his rôles—such as—Josiah Willett, shall we say—'

'Willett!' cried Caroline, Susan and Decima

in chorus. One need not be a regular London theatregoer to know that name.

'Yes, you must make a fair copy of this and send it to him. Yates will find out the direction.'

'But how dare I—He would never read it—'

'Then you will lose nothing. I can promise you that the old man's door mat is knee deep in manuscripts from aspiring dramatists. Why should he not happen to pick up yours—unless his dog chews it up—'

Decima, coming to the table chin on hands, urged: 'Yes, Caroline, you must do that! I will help you to make a copy in my *best* writing. It is the least we can do. And my father would direct it for you. Uncle Tom is right.' To engage in even a one-sided contract with a great actor gave Decima the illusion of being in touch with the theatrical world; nor did she believe that the mighty Willett kept a dog. It was Decima next morning who raided her uncle's office for the best of his paper and pens, and settled Caroline and herself at the table: 'Now, I will begin on Act Two, and you start at the beginning, and you must show me how to lay out the speeches . . .'

To be so industriously engaged served as a distraction from the prevailing indecision, and Susan knew that Caroline had been impressed by Tom's interest and grateful for it. She hinted of this to Tom, who replied shrugging: 'Well, poor girl, she will have a miserable life

124

until she has given this brother an honourable burial in one way or another.' Susan would have agreed, expressing it more delicately, because Caroline had brightened with every inch of progress she had achieved so far in Stephen's service. Susan wondered sometimes what Stephen had been like: totally selfish? Over-indulged in his artistic propensities? She would not dare suggest any of this to Caroline.

A few days of heavy frost kept everyone indoors, busy or idle; Susan found herself avoiding Tom, who seemed on the point of an utterance that he quickly checked; she hoped he was not still planning a wedding journey to the Indies or similar venture. Caroline had a letter from Mr Taplow:

'He tells me he has sold twenty-seven copies of Stephen's book.' She looked round, doleful, thinking no doubt of the outrageous debt owed to her grandfather.

'But that is most promising—for the work of an unknown poet!' declared Tom.

'Is it—really? Mr Taplow does not seem much pleased . . .'

'Never mind Mr Taplow!'

Caroline did not look greatly encouraged by this advice, but she gave a grateful half-smile as she took up her pen to pursue her copying.

Perhaps she did not much mind Mr Taplow, but when on only the following day she received another letter from him, she at once felt apprehensive of fresh trouble.

CHAPTER THIRTEEN

The letter was not from Mr Taplow. It was enclosed in a paper on which was written: 'Mr Taplow regrets his delay in forwarding this missive to Miss Blake.' The writing was of Mr Taplow's clerk, and the said missive was a letter to Caroline from Mr Piper, the old schoolmaster in Dunsyke's village, and directed to Caroline in care of Mr Taplow's office—Why? Yes, she remembered now that a copy of Stephen's book had been sent to Mr Piper from that office, whose address was printed on the flyleaf of the volume—But had she given Mr Piper a direction for herself? She remembered Tom waiting beside her as she scribbled Mr Piper's address; apparently he had had none for her.

This was true, as she saw as soon as she opened the inner letter.

'My dear Caroline—I have received your book of Stephen's poems but before I study them I must give you some news that I cannot send except through the publisher since I have not been sure for some time where a letter would find you.

'I wonder if you know that your grandfather Mr Holroyd died in the week before Christmas. I am sorry to give you the sad news but I do not know of anyone else who could have told you.

'He had been in poor health for several months but would not see the doctor and carried on with his normal activities. His end was sudden and for that we can be thankful. He was attacked in the stable by the stallion Black Roger, and his skull was fractured. The stable boy Albert was witness to the accident and says that the death was instantaneous. Please accept my condolences.

'I write in haste since, as you will understand, affairs here are in some confusion, and you are Mr Holroyd's only surviving relative and consequently the house, grounds, stock and chattels will all be at your disposal. He left no will, but his solicitors and executors are still—as I do not suppose you remember—Cowperthwaite and Watson, 16 Market Square, Skenwith. The younger partner Mr Watson has taken responsibility for the interim, and appointed William Pepper acting farm bailiff. Few of the farm workers were still in their positions, nor has Mr Holroyd retained any of the domestic staff. The condition of the house is therefore poor, and it will require much attention before it is fully habitable. It adds to the difficulty I am afraid that Mr Holroyd recently thought of selling the property, and two purchasers have bid for it, but they are growing impatient and may withdraw if the property is not soon restored to a fair state.

'This will cause you a great deal of trouble but I do hope you can come up here soon and exert the authority that has so suddenly been thrust upon you. I know you will find Mr Watson and Will Pepper very helpful, and I shall be happy to give any assistance I can, although the winter weather limits my movements. I hope to see you soon and I wish you all health and happiness . . .'

As she read the letter, Caroline's face became so white, and her hands trembled so violently as she spread the sheets of the letter on the table, that Susan rose and came to stand beside her; Caroline handed her the letter, saying unsteadily:

'My grandfather is dead.' All she could immediately think of was of bitter, lonely Mr Holroyd, killed in the stable by the stallion who was possibly the same ugly brute of Caroline's memories—She had not dared to enter the stable yard when he was loose. '. . . His end was sudden . . .' Her tears were for that shattering horror, and for the poor boy, watching. Tom meanwhile had come to read over Susan's shoulder, both of them aghast, one-minded. Caroline looked up from one to the other, recollecting: 'But it happened . . . before Christmas!'

'Yet Mr—Piper—says that he writes in haste?' said Susan.

Tom turning over the letter pointed out:

'And so he did; it appears that our friend Taplow has delayed the letter for ... five weeks? Let us hope he does regret it!'

Mr Taplow had in fact slipped the letter into a desk drawer before his own Christmas holiday and it was by mere chance that his clerk had discovered it. The offence did not detain the present company; rather it added urgency to the situation.

'What must Mr Piper be thinking of me!' Caroline cried. 'I must write to him immediately—I must *go* there—'

Lady Bertram noticing the general distress asked: 'What are you all so troubled about, Tom?'

'Caroline has heard that her grandfather has died, ma'am.'

'I did not know that Caroline had a grandfather,' commented Lady Bertram with the mildest of interest.

Decima, who had not known of this either, held out her hand for the letter, with an inquiring glance at Caroline who nodded; everyone could share in the tidings, and Decima, reading, was deeply concerned. She thought: A grandfather of Caroline's must have been *old*, and she cannot have been terribly fond of him; indeed he does not seem to have been a particularly nice old man—*but*, I was right all along: Caroline is a *lady*, and it could be that this 'property' was an establishment of some value, and now she is an heiress, even if the place is become decrepit, and we never knew—It is exciting, like a novel! I am delighted for her! She had more tact than to say so, while Caroline was as fraught and Tom paced the room scowling, turning to ask abruptly:

'Where is this place?'

'It is ... some way west of Aston—on the moors. Skenwith is the nearest sizeable town, in the Eden valley—'

'What can you achieve by travelling all that way now, at this time of year, when your Mr Piper suggests that matters are being more or less coped with? Why not wait till the spring?'

Caroline twisted her hands together and said with a quiet firmness: 'I do not know *how* the people there are coping, and there is the question of the sale, too, if the purchasers will wait, and there might be people there who would remember me and hope I will take an interest ... And perhaps I could help ... I do not know. But, you see, Stephen and I *ran away*.'

'Yes,' said Tom, that habitual dodger of responsibility. 'Yes, I do see that as the owner of the place you have obligations, and even that it could be better to do what can be done promptly, before the spring work can be undertaken. Only, it is a long journey. Who could accompany you? You cannot rely either on your elderly Mr Piper or on what few domestics remain. We do not know what you will find. I would willingly escort you but propriety, as well as anything else, hardly allows it—'

Susan said: 'I will go with you, Caroline.'

There was a silence. It felt like a moment's stupefaction. Tom stared at Susan as if at a stranger; Caroline shook her head but could not speak. Susan went on, in a meek tone that did not conceal her determination:

'I had decided to leave here. You know that. All I could not find was a purpose. Here it is. I wanted to see more of the world and if I can be of use to Caroline I will undertake anything.'

Decima, enthralled, asked: 'And will you come back again?'

Susan smiled, as if that broadened her sense of adventure. 'I do not know. But not for as long as Caroline needs me.'

Caroline was watching Susan, clearly tempted and grateful. Lady Bertram, she had been roused by that silence in the talk, now asked:

'What are you saying? Where do you think of going, Susan?'

'To Dunsyke, ma'am, Caroline's old home in the north—'

'Oh no, you cannot do that. Just you and Caroline? That would be dangerous and imprudent. There will be snow and winds in the north and all manner of dangers. You had better stay at home. Besides I cannot do without you.'

131

She spoke with unusual authority, which served for some reason to provoke Tom to opposition. Striding the room again he proclaimed:

'The scheme is not at all a bad one. The ladies will be good company for one another and will pack enough shawls and thick boots to make themselves comfortable. I will have the travelling carriage oiled and new springs fitted, tomorrow as soon as it is daylight. We shall make up hampers of food. And Culthorpe shall take them. He and his nephew, that strong ox of a lad who could pull a carriage out of any snowdrift. Culthorpe is a Yorkshireman and afraid of nothing. He knows rough country and knows his horses and will have the whole expedition there and back safe.'

This made the whole escapade sound like a summer picnic. Tom's motives were mixed: He longed to please Susan and to show that he would yield to her in her wish for freedom; he felt a true pity for Miss Blake and was offering her, between Susan and Culthorpe, the best support he could. He revelled in his own generosity and to his mother's continued protests could say briskly: 'Come now, Mama, you will have Decima here to sit with you for a few days; are we not lucky that she has not gone back to town!' This too appeased Decima, who hitherto had been longing to return to town and to escape her grandmother's needlework; but now she felt useful and in a good cause—for a few days.

Because Tom's air of command kept everything running to and fro; because the departure took place in a misty dawn; because the travelling carriage with its freshly polished accoutrements was an unfamiliar sight—the Bertrams had rarely made long journeys—and Culthorpe in his greatcoat was a strange dignitary; because it was scarcely more than thirty-six hours since Caroline had received the letter from Mr Piper; because of all this, she and Susan had had no opportunity to discuss or appreciate whither they were travelling or why. Perhaps as the carriage rolled out of the main gates of the park, each had a waking moment of doubt, and unformed query; they turned to each other in smiling reassurance as both received it. Only Decima had sped them, running after the carriage from the doorsteps and calling: 'How I wish I were coming with you!'

To be envied by Decima was some touch of encouragement. Caroline looking out at the dimly brightening day was somehow surprised to see the landscape still normal—the farms, the leafless copses, standing in their accustomed places in what felt like a dream-world. At the top of a rise, Culthorpe's nephew Dick leapt from the box and ran into a farm gateway, whistling as if in signal, to return with an element of reality: a long-legged collie dog dragged on a length of twine.

'One of my father's yard dogs,' he introduced them as he opened the door of the carriage. 'Uncle Amos thought happen we'd need to have the carriage guarded. He says please to let him ride in with you till he understands what he's to do. But I wouldn't touch him till he knows you.'

The dog showed wicked yellow teeth in an unfriendly grin. 'What is his name?' asked Susan drawing back her feet.

'Rightly I don't know, Miss Price.' He threw a piece of sacking on to the floor and pushed the dog on to it with his foot. 'He gets just "the hound". Later he can run alongside. Lie down now—' he admonished the dog, who resignedly obeyed and showed no alarm as the carriage was set in motion again.

'Good morning, Hound,' Susan addressed him. A glint of one eye briefly answered her. 'You see—He knows me already . . .' A human element, as it were, had been added to the situation; their journey gained momentum though as yet no clear purpose. The minds of both dwelt on Mansfield Park: Had they escaped, or basely fled? To have quit the house before Lady Bertram was awake was enough prick at the conscience.

In any case, they could not usefully plan ahead. All depended on their finding this Mr Watson and hearing what he had to tell them. Meanwhile the steady speed of the carriage insisted that Culthorpe had matters in hand

and was as steady of purpose. As the mist was dispersed by a cold wind, and the miles passed, widening the distance behind them, perforce Susan and Caroline had patiently to admit that they were committed to their enterprise and its unknown nature. If Susan felt a measure of relief in escaping—yes, that had to be the word—her life of servitude at Mansfield; and if Caroline too was relieved of the position of hanger-on—which had troubled her however kind everyone had been to her—among the Bertram and Yates families, it was evident only in an increased readiness to smile, to comment on the passing landscape and settle to travelling. It is always, on any journey a comfort to be *off*, to be on the way at last, to be sure of congenial company and to have left everyone else behind.

So Susan and Caroline passed a happy day. Time enough to deal with Mr Watson when they met him; the weather remained clear, and Culthorpe and Tom between them had planned a route along the roads most likely to be direct and unencumbered by traffic. On the first day, they had made such good progress that Culthorpe in twilight lit the carriage lamps and they rolled on for some time in the dark. Other lighted vehicles passed them; once a stagecoach rattled by, and Caroline looked sympathetically at the poor figures muffled-up on its roof. So, she suddenly remembered, had she and Stephen travelled on their runaway journey. To be so cherished in her present conveyance—again, indebted to the Bertrams.—made her uneasy. She remarked on this to Susan later, as they sat by the parlour fire of a coaching inn; and Susan said casually:

'Perhaps when you know the terms of your grandfather's will, you will find that you can afford a carriage of your own.'

'I had not thought of that,' Caroline excaimed. Indeed she had not. She had not thought out the possibilities at all, but had felt somehow that her grandfather, never providing money in life, would be as unyielding in death. Thinking of it now, she said: 'I do not expect he has left any money. If the property is so run down, it cannot be worth anything; besides, why should he have wanted to sell it, if not for his immediate needs?'

'True,' said Susan, yawning. The topic did not detain them. Mr Watson was still in the non-existent future.

'Ah well . . .' Caroline murmured. 'We shall see.'

Soon the four of them had formed a close and friendly group, as they travelled through what felt like a limbo in time. Susan had been afraid of Culthorpe in her first days at Mansfield, when he gave her riding lessons of unsparing severity; but now she found him very affable, even avuncular. Dick was always kind and cheerful. It certainly cheered Susan to be

136

free of the disapproval which everyone at Mansfield—even her own sister—had lately shown her; Susan the good, clever and helpful, had not taken that at all well. But now, no one cared; all that concerned them was the weather, the state of the near lead horse's knee, the how-many-miles calculations and day-to-day practicalities.

In the thin shelter of a wood Culthorpe drew up while he and Dick conferred about that horse's knee. Susan and Caroline alighted, to admire the view below the road in a brief gleam of sunlight, while Hound who preferred to ride ('And no wonder of that, if some ladies feed him *biscuits!*' as Dick pointed out) remained in the carriage. On a sudden a horrific tumult, as if of a whole pride of bloodthirsty lions, broke out and they swung round to see a ragged boy fleeing for his life into the wood. He had come up on the off side and peered into the carriage to see what he might steal, not expecting Hound's reception. Hound was off into the wood in pursuit and came back reluctantly to Dick's whistle, grinning widely.

'I understand now what you mean about guarding the carriage,' Susan, pale-cheeked, said to Culthorpe.

'May I give him a biscuit *now*?' pleaded Caroline.

'Aye, that's right, make him into a lapdog like one of her ladyship's pugs.'

137

Such excitement enlivened their days but there were no serious delays or mishaps: Gales blew down a tree and blocked a road, and there was an insalubrious inn where rats gnawed Caroline's leather valise during the night, but the weather held, apart from showers and gusts. There were variations in the scenery as they passed through sleepy market towns, the gritty villages of the coalfields, valleys with stark mill buildings; and at last, after a snow shower that left the undulating skyline whitened and rising, Caroline observed in a tone of apprehension and some regret:

'There are the moors . . .'

CHAPTER FOURTEEN

Once again the domestic circle at Mansfield Park was suddenly depleted. Lady Bertram lamented hourly the absence of Susan, and almost as often that of Miss Blake. At every gust of cold wind, or flake of snow, she shook her head and remarked in a plaintive tone: 'I warned them, you know—I warned them that this was no weather for travelling. I expect they will have to turn back.' To this hope she clung as the travellers did not reappear; she showed no further interest in their affairs.

Decima was in similar case, except that she

did not suppose there would be any turning back. Her excitement over the change in Caroline's prospects faded as the slow days passed; Decima had no place in the story; Tom had required her to bear her grandmother company 'for a few days'—but Decima had not reckoned with the length of the journey, nor had she any idea of the time it might take to deal with matters in that frozen north; and what indeed if Susan, as had been hinted, did not come back to Mansfield—and nor might Caroline? Here was Decima, supporting unsupported her grandmother; if her residence at Mansfield since Christmas had been in the way of a punishment, it now threatened to become a life sentence. She was fond of her grandmother but did not find constant attendance on her fulfilling to romantic aspirations. Nor did her Uncle Tom play the part of a rejected lover requiring consolation; he was always in a bad temper because his foxhunting was curtailed by sodden earth or lame horses. Decima's spirits sank so low that she forgot all about Signor Lasso, and about the little party that was to have been given for her in town to mark her coming-out. Her mother wrote:

'. . . You are a very good girl, my dear, to stay and look after your Grandmama while Susan is away. It will give Susan a chance to decide what to do with her life. It would not be wise of her to marry Tom—do you not agree—

and it would be difficult for her to stay on at Mansfield if she did not. I do not believe Caroline will stay either at Mansfield or with us in town—why should she, now that she has a house of her own! But I hope you will meet her again. You can imagine what frenzy there is here, since "The Duke" was abandoned and we are to toss together a series of "Shakespeare recitals"—I wish you could be here for these and I would myself rather be at Mansfield than in town for the next few weeks!'

That Caroline might pass out of her life deepened Decima's gloom; she had not thought of that. Susan, whatever her future course of life, was still a cousin and should be in touch. Julia added that John Yates would undertake to place 'The Death of Wisdom' in the way of Josiah Willett, but did not hold out any hope; the mighty Willett at present was on tour on the south coast as Shylock. Decima had the negative comfort of knowing that she had done her best to help Caroline over the verse drama at least: She had finished their fair copy, packed it most neatly, and sent it already to her father in town; but that left only another gap in her life, something else to wait for and more leisure to devote to her grandmother's embroidery. She was surprisingly pleased when, on a rainy midday, the servant announced that Mr Rushworth had called. His amiable dull visage looked like that of an old friend.

Lady Bertram too roused herself to acquaint Mr Rushworth with the absence of Miss Price and Miss Blake, who had set out on a perilous journey against her own advice, but who would arrive back on any day. His gaze of horror and bewilderment transferred itself to Decima for some elaboration of the tale, and she told him that the two ladies had set out for the house of Miss Blake's grandfather in Cumberland and had by now very probably arrived there.

'I did not know that Miss Blake had a grandfather.'

'Well, she has not, because he is dead. That is why she has been sent for.'

'Oh, I am sorry to hear that.'

Discretion did not come naturally to Decima at any time—indeed it was she who had divulged to Mr Rushworth the state of Caroline's affairs and inspired his gesture towards the publication of the poetry book; and today she was mildly exhilarated to have someone free to talk to, so prattled on:

'I do not know that Caroline was so very sorry to hear of it. I do not know that they had had anything to do with each other since she and Stephen left home. She never spoke of him. But, you see, he had no other relatives, so that is why Caroline had to go up there so promptly. We do not know what there will be, to inherit, but it seems it will be all for

141

Caroline. It is rather romantic, do you not feel that? I am longing to know what happens, and surely, she will write to us?'

From the confused solemnity of Mr Rushworth's countenance, he was not affected by the romantic aspect of her account. 'So she has gone to see to all these serious legal questions for herself?'

'But Susan has gone with her—'

'Miss Price?' he asked, sharply.

'Yes—Susan,' insisted Decima, reflecting that he was slow to take a meaning. She made little allowance for his having been away since before Christmas, and in ignorance of all news of Mansfield Park. 'Susan went because she thinks of going away in any case. You see, Tom asked her to marry him, but she refused him.'

Lady Bertram, excluded from their conversation, had fallen into a doze from which she now roused again to say:

'Mr Rushworth, Tom will be sorry to have missed you. He has gone out hunting.'

'He will be back early, on such a day,' Decima suggested. 'So he can tell you about it himself, if you will wait an hour—'

She had not found Mr Rushworth a responsive audience—he sat there in increasing stupefaction—but this last notion put him to instant flight. He bowed his farewells with scarcely an excuse and left, to ride home through the rain that had marred Tom's hunting, not anxious to encounter Tom in the mood that that would have caused, and certainly not to invite discussion of Tom's private life. 'I would not know what to say,' James told himself, 'and I do not know what to think . . .' He did not altogether trust Tom Bertram at best, nor was it unusual to him to find himself bereft of words or of thoughts; it was his own feelings that were in uproar, and these he was not accustomed to consider. He had not known that he *had* such feelings until he had become involved again with the Bertram people and nor could he remember how that had come about. He had looked forward, during the tedious weeks in Bath, to visiting Mansfield Park again and felt now only cold, wet and lonely as he approached Sotherton.

Decima on that evening found Tom's mood trying. Very well, he had had no hunting, but why should he scowl and speak to no one? While Decima played a Field nocturne on the pianoforte—producing on her grandmother the effect of a lullaby—Tom sat at the end of the room reading, never raising his eyes from his book. Curious to know what he had found so absorbing Decima finally looked over his shoulder; the book was one of Sir Thomas's, entitled: 'The Harvesting and Rendering of Sugar Cane'. Forgetful of the Jamaican estates, she did not deduce that Tom meant to visit Antigua after all; she was afraid his wits were wandering, and dared not speak. But at bed time, as she started up the stairs, he called her back:

'Decima: I am going up to town tomorrow, I have decided. I wish you would see that the roan mare has exercise.'

'Demoiselle!' cried Decima, sounding as slow as Mr Rushworth. She leaned over the banister to add: 'Do you not expect Susan to come back, then?'

'That has nothing to do with it. Tell Culthorpe—Oh, the d—take it, he is away—Tell the stables that I said so. I expect I shall be at Julia's.' He stalked away down the passage, muttering what sounded like: '. . . All so foolish and unnecessary . . .'

Decima was not sorry to be without him when he had gone—presumably to Marylebone—but loneliness deepened. Even her cousins Mary and Frances from the Parsonage were both at school in Bedford since the new year. Decima meanwhile should have been 'out' by now, a young lady about town, instead of being in the sole company of an elderly widow in her mourning—though self-pity threatened when Decima reflected on this; she tried to ignore it.

Lady Bertram took Tom's departure serenely. 'I expect he is gone to bring Susan and Caroline home,' she remarked. 'That is wise of him, because do you see those heavy dark clouds beyond the woods? I am afraid we are going to have deep snow.'

144

CHAPTER FIFTEEN

Darkness had fallen when the carriage finally entered the town of Skenwith and Caroline was glad of it. The closer she approached the end of the journey, the more her trepidation gripped her. As she recognised parts of the landscape she became more unwilling to do so; she was being drawn back into a life willingly forgotten; it forced upon her, painfully, a sense of shame. She had run away. In all the time of her absence she had not admitted that. But indeed the time had not been long, and she was in danger of being thrown back into her memories—and the memories of other people—to the destruction of the new *persona* that she now felt she had created in the south. Even Susan could not save her. As if for the first time Caroline was stricken by the loss of her mother and of Stephen. An empty and hostile world enclosed her. The local people—rigid in their obedience to family duty—would blame her for abandoning her poor old grandfather and suspect her—again, according to their tenets—of living a wanton if not shameful life in the frivolous south. She had lost the commitment to Stephen's poetry that had sustained her, when she now contemplated her situation without him. What was poetry?

Susan observed most of this from Caroline's manner, adding to it the fatigue of the journey and the unwelcome prospect; she hoped that a night's rest and her own cheerful company would restore Caroline and prepare her to meet Mr Watson tomorrow. The Crown Inn at Skenwith was warm and homely enough to relieve depression; and Susan could see, by morning, that Caroline was eager, if gloomily, to start on her duties, if merely for distraction. They sent to ask whether Mr Watson would receive them, and he offered to do so immediately, and they crossed the Market Square, under a scattering of snow that might have disappointed Lady Bertram, and were conducted into a tidy office with a blazing fire on its hearth where Mr Watson, a young man with a welcoming smile, rose to greet them.

The smile was sincere. Henry Watson was a local man, though he had pursued his legal studies in Halifax. He was well informed on the local gossip and had had some curiosity about the elusive heiress of the old curmudgeon up at Dunsyke; she had left before he took up his position in the firm, and as he fussed about, arranging chairs, he liked what he saw: She was entirely correct, very handsome in a neat fashion, and had brought a chaperone.

'I am so glad you are come, Miss Blake,' he began. 'It is good of you to travel north at this

146

time of year and I hope we need not detain
'If you please,' she interrupted quietly. 'I
would first of all like to hear about the . . .
about his burial . . .'

'Yes, yes. Certainly,' said Henry Watson, a
little abashed. 'He was placed in the Holroyd
family vault, here in Skenwith, in St Olaf's
churchyard.'

'Yes. Thank you.' Her mother, she too
clearly remembered, had been placed apart, in
a grave below a knotty yew tree. And
Stephen's grave was a pauper's. 'I shall visit it.
I must visit the house too. Is anyone living in it
now?'

'Yes, an elderly couple occupy it, though I
am afraid the building is in a poor state. We—
subject to your approval—are paying a small
sum to Mr and Mrs Barber to act as
caretakers—'

'Meggie!' exclaimed Caroline, her cheeks
flushing.

'I beg your pardon?'

'Meggie—Mrs Barber—was our nurse. My
brother's and mine. Jack Barber was the
groom.'

'Quite so. I am afraid there are no horses
there now.'

'Black Roger?' asked Caroline, urgently.

'The stallion who . . .'

'Yes—'

'He was destroyed,' said Henry Watson
simply.

'Good,' said Caroline, nodding. It seemed to Susan that a short pause between the other

two indicated more reverence for a death than would be accorded to that of Mr Holroyd. Cynicism apart, Susan was pleased by Caroline's reviving energy. Perhaps it was doing her good to have come here and to deal with her memories. By now she had established quite close terms with Mr Watson and was raising another subject that must have been worrying her.

'. . . You see, my grandfather paid for my brother's education but my brother was to pay him back, when he was earning, but he never did and so I felt obliged to—but of course I could not; if when one dies someone owes a debt, does it still have to be paid? I never knew whether it was written down, formally . . . I am not being clear!'

Mr Watson smiled broadly. 'Supposing you pay a sum into your grandfather's estate now, what happens? The whole estate devolves upon you, so you have it back again. That is clear to me.'

Caroline's sigh of relief was profound and unsteady. 'But is there any estate?' she inquired without perceptible interest. They were at least, it seemed, coming to deal practically with the topic of money, where Mr Watson had begun the interview.

He took up a folder of documents from his desk and cleared his throat. 'Your grandfather had made few investments and at the time of his death was owing an amount that will be difficult to reckon up, for household bills, wages to his employees, and maintenance of the buildings of the farms. He had been heedless too of collecting the rents of his tenants, so there could be money to retrieve there. However, he owned a great deal of land, some of it non-productive under his management but potentially valuable. And the house at Dunsyke is of some historical interest. You will know that he had considered selling the house, with or without its grounds? I must put you in touch with the agent who hopes to arrange about that—a very vigorous character, Arthur Brough—a cousin of mine actually—who has some ideas on the subject. I am supposing that you do not intend to live in the house yourself?' And when Caroline denied it with vehemence he went on: 'I am supposing though that you would wish to examine the house's contents. Jack Barber has tried to tidy the place and has locked away various items that must be valuable, some dating back to before your grandfather's time. As well, there are items of a personal nature, perhaps possessions of your own that you left behind—'

Caroline perceptibly winced. 'No, I think not, but I agree that it is my duty to sort through it all. And I must see Meggie. And Mr Piper. And if, Mr Watson, you could give a message to your cousin . . . ?'

'I look forward to seeing the house,' Susan put in. 'Is it far away—within walking distance?'

'Not conveniently,' Mr Watson told her. 'But we shall find you transport!'

Susan mentioned to Caroline: 'Dick says the farrier wants that horse to rest for three days, so we could not in any case start back.'

'In any case,' appended Mr Watson, shaking his head, 'it begins to seem that you will need to remain here for more than three days.'

Neither lady protested. When they left Mr Watson, they emerged into a town that had become friendly and unhurried of a sudden. They set out before noon, in a small wooden farm-cart drawn by a small stout fell pony, driven by a bootboy from the Crown Inn, on their local engagements. There was no more snow; the ground was icy in places but a whipping breeze stirred the clouds aside as they made for the moors and Dunsyke.

The hamlet of Dunsyke itself, where Mr Piper had lived since his retirement, was a cluster of stone cottages at the foot of the gill dropping from the upper levels. His little schoolhouse was here, and a bridge across the river. His daughter who kept house for him cried: 'Why Caroline—Father *will* be pleased!' when she opened the door; she ran to provide elderberry wine and lardy-cake, while her

150

father was discovered at the fireside with 'Poems of Stephen Blake' in his hands.

'No, this is not for show!' he assured Caroline, chuckling. 'I heard you were in the town, but I am spending a deal of time with this little book. Has your forgetful publisher told you, Caroline, how well it has been received in these parts? Local poets are often highly thought of for that reason alone, but these are valued for their quality. Arthur Brough, the agent, wanted a copy when he knew he might meet you, and he had to send as far as Carlisle, where there were only two copies to be had. Now, just see that your man is ready to prepare a second edition, I promise you it will be needed and will last for a good while as the critics catch on.'

'I will tell Mr Taplow,' said Caroline, delighted. 'Though I do not expect he will obey me.'

'Tell Tom to tell him,' Susan suggested. 'That worked last time.'

Caroline noticed in passing that Susan still spoke of Tom in her normal easy manner; they had not spoken of his rejected proposal, and Caroline occasionally wondered what Susan truly felt about it. Herself in emotional turmoil today, she was the more admiring of Susan's cheerful composure. 'I am so *glad* you came with me,' she cried to the astonished Susan, who had engaged in a discussion with Mr Piper on the poetry of Coleridge.

'We shall have you here for a while, now you are come?' Mr Piper said. 'You must have missed the countryside.'

'I have. But we are now on our way up to the house, to see what should be done about it, and to see Meggie and Jack.'

'Aye, well . . . It is a shame about that house, that's all. But you must not let it upset you. It's for you to please yourself now.'

After that cryptic advice Caroline and Susan remounted their cart and proceeded round the flank of the moor, climbing, the track growing steeper and rougher, until it converged with the beck at a lip in the ground whence the shoulders of moorland fell back to form a deep corrie, across whose bowl Dunsyke House regarded them. Its back to a wall of crags, encircled by banks of heather, it was exquisitely placed; it had been, perhaps by the late Mr Holroyd's grandfather in the middle of the last century, re-faced in the local sandstone that glowed the more richly for its drab surroundings and was carved in a Palladian style as foreign to those, but altogether impressive in this spot.

'But it is beautiful!' Susan exclaimed. 'A miniature palace—yet so simple! You must have loved living here.'

Perhaps that was tactless, but Caroline disregarded it. And as the track circled the tufty swamp of the bowl, and the house drew nearer, all too unattractive was a foreground of broken fences, tumbled walls, tattered gale-blown trees clawing with their roots at the sky. The track avoided the front entrance with its flight of steps and led round to a side door, probably the only one in use nowadays. Caroline was out of the cart instantly, calling: 'Meggie!' as she pushed open the creaking door; Susan followed after a prudent interval, into a large kitchen lighted by one candle, where Caroline was already in the embrace of a small woman in a sacking apron that covered a neat white pinafore, a shawl round her shoulders, who was calling to the boy of the cart: 'Bobby! Away and find Jack—This is Caroline come home!'

Here there was blackberry wine and gingerbread, impeccably served on china plates of varying design. Susan suspected that it was in this kitchen that the Barbers lived; she glimpsed a bed behind a curtain in a far corner. Meggie, apologising, threw off the sacking apron; she had been preparing to feed the hens, and thrust her bucket behind an oak settle. '. . . Yes, the hens do us well enough, my dear, and Jack has the old side lawn for potatoes . . .'

'But, Meggie, can we not find you a cottage nearer the town—It is so cold and lonely up here—'

Jack, who had entered, said: 'Nay now, we're here to take care of the house, and it's needed—There's so many things are of value amid the rubbish still. I'll show you what I've got locked up in the chest in the west attic— One thing, your grandad grew worried about thieves and he'd hide things every-peculiar-where—Meggie only the other day counted twenty gold sovereigns among a jar of old horse pills—'

'And those old pictures he hid in the old hayloft—Ruined they were, when its roof fell in!' sighed Meggie.

Susan and Caroline glanced at each other in some dismay. The vagaries of Mr Holroyd multiplied upon them and threatened to consume time as well as effort. This preoccupied them when they were back in the Crown, where Mr Watson had left a message telling them that his cousin Mr Brough was out of town but would wait upon Miss Blake in the course of a few days. 'What are we to do about Culthorpe and Dick?' Caroline wondered. 'How long are they to wait here? It would be foolish to send the carriage back empty to Mansfield.'

Culthorpe, summoned, said that he had merely been told to bring the ladies to Skenwith and, by implication, to bring them back. He was not complaining; he was happy to have a holiday in his native north country and cared only for the wellbeing of his horses. He hinted, too, that for Miss Blake to arrive in an equipage like his had done her no harm among the local populace.

This was true. The neighbourhood might have expected the worst of the old man's errant granddaughter, but that had been largely in the hope of sensing scandal, and when she turned out to be so entirely respectable they were not disappointed, but showed a more friendly interest. Caroline, sensing that, was already almost at home among them and Mansfield by comparison was further away. However long it might take her, her first duty was here. But Susan . . .

'I shall stay as long as you do,' said Susan firmly. 'I suppose we must write to Tom and ask for instructions. We were bound to write to my aunt today, were we not, to say that we have arrived safely. Are we in time for the post? Do you write to Tom—It was to you that he lent the carriage, you see—and I will write to Aunt Bertram and Decima. And we must hurry, if you wish to visit the churchyard before dark.'

The principle, if any, that influenced Susan's not writing to Tom did not detain Caroline, and the letters were hastily written and despatched, and she and Susan wrapped themselves in their carriage cloaks and walked through gathering dusk to the churchyard. The visit to the family vault was something of a formality, but Caroline lingered for so long at her mother's grave that Susan waiting by the gate was afraid she would grow chilled. When she rejoined Susan, it was with a new air of purpose that she said:

'I know that my mother would have hated to see Dunsyke in such disgraceful disrepair and Meggie and Jack strugging as they are to keep it in some kind of order. I must try to help them.' Smiling a little she added: 'And who knows, we might find gold coins in the root cellar.'

It required no such inducement to make Susan eager too to set the house in order. 'Indeed, where can we begin? It is all so cold and so dark—'

'We shall be able to find help. The chief thing is, that we must not let Meggie and Jack feel we are dissatisfied with all their hard work—far beyond them as the task has been.'

'We might explain to them that the place must be tidied up for the potential buyers—whom I expect Mr Watson's cousin will be the one to tell us of?'

Mr Watson's cousin did. He was a plump and enthusiastic man, younger again than his cousin, and as soon as they had accepted chairs in his office he began to stride up and down, waving his podgy hands and declaiming.

'I believe in looking forward,' he pronounced. 'I have worked in Manchester and Leeds and several of your great industrial cities. I have taken the pulse of our nation and I can forecast the fashion of its development.

What do I see, as I look ahead? I see a great expansion of trade and of productivity, under many enterprising citizens who are amassing wealth on a scale as yet unknown. And what do these captains of industry see fit to do with their money? They aspire to emulate those who previously led the country in manners and style of life. They build for themselves splendid mansions in their cities but after that, what? They build themselves mansions in the country, with deer parks and fountains and turrets, and what do they do in their country estates, in emulation of the country squires they have superseded? In more and more cases they pursue *sport*!'

He brought out that last word with a climactic triumph that made Susan and Caroline, dazzled by his rhetoric, blink in silence. Then he approached the table, drew out a chair and sat down, continuing in a normally conversational voice:

'Now I will tell you what we shall do. You must tell me if you disagree. Sport: That is the objective of the affluent citizen. And what we have here, up at Dunsyke, is a perfect example of the country estate for a rich townsman. A house of quality—an excellent situation—open countryside—countless acres of rough shooting—or hunting—all he could want. Now this is how we shall be clever. We shall find a buyer of *taste*—Not some jumped-up manufacturer of spinning machinery but a man

157

of vision who would perceive the possibilities of the property yet wish to make his own mark upon it. I know that the place is in poor condition but, believe me, it would cost you more to render it habitable than you would lose by selling it to our man of taste at what we shall call a give-away price—and so, fifty years on, it would be; looking forward, I am certain that this man's grandchildren will say: "But Grandpapa, is *that* all you paid for this magnificent estate!" and he will say: "Yes, my dears, I secured it at a knock-down price from a lady who had no idea of its true value; I am afraid her agent cheated her".'

He smiled from one to the other of the ladies in such a winning manner that they could have taken the notion of his cheating Caroline as a joke. Susan observed:

'Your scheme depends perhaps on your finding your industrialist of taste. And perhaps on what your chosen give-away price will be.'

Ruffling the pages of a ledger Mr Brough told her: 'I have had two clients on my books since last September, but I ceased to seek any after Mr Holroyd's death since I knew nothing of the wishes—or existence—of any heir. One potential buyer is a gentleman from the Border who intends to extend the sheep-farming business that Mr Holroyd had, by default, discontinued. He plans to rebuild all the stock buildings on a larger scale, and to purchase two of the farms adjoining your property, and to breed sheep and horses. The house, he says "can stay where it is".' Mr Brough glanced up at them, inscrutably non-commenting. 'He offers a munificent price, let me mention, but what he desires is the stretch of land. And here I have a Mr Trotter, owner of a prosperous glassworks near Manchester, who is in search of the type of rustic family seat that I spoke of. He was much taken with the house when I showed him, from the head of the approach and moreover he evinced no ambitions for its improvement. I murmured something about an ornamental lake and formal gardens but he said: "Nay, it needs none of that fussy stuff up here." Now I must divulge to you the bids that both these clients have made.' He did so, naming first a sum that both Susan and Caroline assumed to be that of the munificent sheep-breeder, until he followed it with another of colossal size, proving the first sum to be the 'give-away' price. They looked at each other in faint horror.

'Now, you wish to discuss all this together and I will not hurry you. You should ask to see the accounts of the estate—the outgoings, the rents—to arrive at a valuation, but . . .'

'But we are told that such records have lapsed recently,' Caroline supplied. 'Miss Price, however, has experience of these matters. She has helped her uncle with the running of his estate for many years.'

Mr Brough looked with approval on Miss Price. 'Is it the opinion of this meeting then,' he asked with his winning smile, 'that I write to Mr Trotter and re-open negotiations?'

It was. 'I like the sound of Mr Trotter,' Susan announced. It was with his money, rather than with the man, that the vendors should be concerned, but Mr Brough did not point that out. Ladies so often showed a feminine turn of mind, but why not; these two appeared cool-headed enough and he should have no trouble with them.

'It has been a pleasure,' he elaborated on that sentiment as he escorted them out.

'So now,' said Caroline as they crossed the now familiar Market Square, 'our work begins.'

CHAPTER SIXTEEN

Their work now, of course, was principally in the sorting of the smaller and more personal items and effects from the house. For Caroline this was sometimes painful, sometimes distasteful, but now and then rewarding, in that a tangible reminder of her mother or of Stephen could enable her to feel that they too were being set free of the house's bondage and unhappy associations.

Up at the house, work was going on apace.

The air rang with the whacking of axes as the local labour recruited by Jack Barber disposed of the brokendown sheep pens and stables. Possibly Mr Trotter would have a use for the better pieces of furniture, but some could be whacked up for firewood, or hauled down to go to the sale rooms of Skenwith or Carlisle—'While we are not snowed in,' as Jack Barber prudently mentioned; but the snow blew away in the wind before it settled; and there were leaves showing on the elder bush in the corner of the inn yard.

Dick had carried sackfuls of what looked like rubbish down to the Crown, where Caroline and Susan might sort it in the warmth of their room. It was a tedious task but, mindful of gold sovereigns, they went about it patiently. Caroline discovered in a bundle of rags a locket that she had seen her mother wear; whose was the lock of hair, soft as a baby's, within it? Meanwhile Susan was wiping the dust off an account book, saying: 'Now this may be useful . . .' Mr Holroyd, they had been told, had quarrelled with and dismissed his steward some while ago; but when she opened the book, out fell only a shower of paper scraps; mice had removed the contents to make nests. Susan was amused.

'An excellent specimen of accountancy!' she declared. 'Even Tom does not allow his books to get into this condition. I should send this to him, for encouragement!'

'It is strange that we have not yet heard from him.' Caroline recollected, snapping shut the locket.

'Well, but we have not heard from anyone, for that matter, and I for one am not troubled.' Busy they were, but perhaps they both still revelled in their freedom, and allowed themselves to be preoccupied. Had they thought of it they might have guessed that with Lady Bertram's lassitude, Decima's sulkiness at her captivity, and the crises in town over the Orion, no one was particularly anxious to hear what went on at Dunsyke; but, about Tom? Caroline on impulse asked:

'You wish to have . . . nothing to do with Tom now?'

Susan considered at some length before she replied: 'Yes, I do feel he will come to see that it was wrong. The idea of our marrying I mean. It will be better not to let him discuss it. Mostly it is his pride that will not let him admit it, and only he can deal with that.'

'Oh, I hope you are right. I think you are. Because he is a kind and gentle person at heart.'

'You think so too?' said Susan, not surprised. 'I suppose I cannot avoid him for the rest of my life—But we shall have to see what happens . . . At the moment I am more interested by the prospect of meeting Mr Trotter.'

This significant encounter was to take place

on the very next day. The client had assured Mr Brough promptly that he was indeed still interested in Dunsyke House and wished to hasten up from his glassworks to examine the property more closely. Mr Brough told the ladies that this was promising but warned them that according to the rules of the game Mr Trotter on this occasion would find all manner of faults in order to reduce the price. Mr Brough would borrow a suitable vehicle to convey his client up the rough track and hoped to convey the ladies at the same time—if the snow held off . . .

That evening, in the diningroom of the Crown, the ladies glimpsed a stranger whom they both decided must be Mr Trotter. He was stout and red-faced and shouted at the waiter, about some omission; the waiter and the ladies, quailed at his voice; Caroline confessed that she did not now look forward to their meeting. Susan said:

'Let us set out very early, and walk up to the house. It is not far. I am afraid we might say the wrong things—we had much better leave him to Mr Brough.' And as the morning was fair, they agreed that they would enjoy the walk, and that they were being diplomatic rather than cowardly. They sent a message to Mr Brough and were out of the town before sunrise.

'Stephen used to say, when he came to school,' Caroline remembered, 'that it took him half an hour down and an hour up again. I would come to meet him, but not at such a speed. Some of the pupils came on their ponies ...' She turned back to look at the view, tying her shawl closer about her shoulders. 'How I wish,' she suddenly cried, 'that I could see it again in summer, with the bilberries ripe and the rabbits scuttering about—'

'Would you like to live here?' Susan suggested.

'Do you know,' admitted Caroline wondering. 'I do love this country. I had forgotten. If there were no one to be afraid of ... Meggie was telling me that there will be a cottage for sale, just above Mr Piper's. It has a garden—even a little orchard—'

'Oh, let me share it with you! We shall be two happy old maids in mittens, sitting in our doorway watching the world go by—'

From this idyllic picture they were roused only by the necessity of outstripping Mr Trotter; they reached the house in time to warn Meggie of that gentleman's approach, speaking of him as if he were Attila the Goth. Meggie was unterrified.

'Nay, if he likes the house, he's all right. And we've got it all tidy for him.' The exaggeration was excusable, in view of the toil Meggie and her strong village girls had exerted indoors; but the state of the whole property now would bear inspection as would not have seemed possible a few weeks ago.

Susan and Caroline had had no acquaintance among industrial magnates but could postulate that it was characteristic in them to talk loudly even when not angry. When Mr Trotter heard that the two of them had walked up from the town that morning he slapped his knees and roared with laughter, shouting: '*My* girls would never have done that! It's "Dada, we must have the carriage" all the time'—and at his squeaky mockery of his daughters' voices Mr Brough too had to laugh. The two gentlemen set off on a long survey of the grounds whence Mr Trotter's bellowed queries and comments echoed back to the house; when they returned he wanted Caroline to answer a few queries about the house as she remembered living in it; then to her surprise he drew her apart, into the alcove of the main staircase, and brought from his pocket a small dark green volume that made her heart leap as he said in a moderated voice:

'Look here. Brough showed me this book. It's a book of poems and he says they were written in this house? Eh?'

'Yes, sir. They were written by my brother.'

'Well I never. How often do you find a house a poet lived in? That would add a bit to the price; eh?' He accompanied the last interjection by a solemn wink. Caroline began to like Mr Trotter. Fingering the pages he went on:

'Poems about this countryside too. I must

read them some time. But I'll tell you what I'd want to do if I buy the house. It's still "if", mind you, but I'd want to lay in a stock of these neat little books to give to my friends when they come visiting. How would I get them? Send to this man in London—This address? Or send round the bookshops? Do they have bookshops round here?'

Caroline remembering Mr Piper's advice recommended Mr Trotter to apply to Mr Taplow; if anyone could speed a second printing of 'Poems of Stephen Blake' out of Mr Taplow, Mr Trotter was more likely to achieve it than she—or even than Tom. Susan when she heard of all this echoed Caroline's hope that Mr Trotter would become the next owner of Dunsyke; and Mr Brough, when the client had finally departed, conceded that they might be a *little* hopeful of it.

'He will think of some sudden drawback and threaten to drop out, to see if I will drop my price. I will tell him that I *may* have another client in mind who will meet it. Then presently he will send a surveyor of his own—some mean-minded little Mancunian who will spend many days in counting all the wormholes in the beams—Well, you see how it goes along. What I intended to say to you is that your assistance in the clearing of the house has been inestimably useful, and I am most grateful. Now I feel that I may not need to trespass on your time and goodwill for long just now.

166

Meanwhile you will have matters still to settle with Henry Watson but he is bound by the law's delays. And we will bid Jack Barber's gang of stalwarts carry on the demolishing of the old farm buildings. They appear to be enjoying the work, anyway.'

It had not escaped Caroline and Susan that Mr Brough found a certain enjoyment in his own work and his manipulation of the 'rules of the game'. The ethics of these they could not assess, but they trusted him. When he turned to Caroline and said very gravely: 'You do appreciate Miss Blake, do you not, that by one way and another you have come into possession of a quite considerable fortune?' she thanked him as if by his genius alone Dunsyke had been raised phoenix-like from its ashes of squalor. There were still many details to be attended to but it began to seem that their immediate task was ending and they might leave Mr Brough and Mr Trotter to one another, which would be a great relief; what they did not yet consider was the employment of a new phase of freedom. An unexpected letter addressed to them both did thrust this question upon them:

My dear Miss Price and Miss Blake,
I was disappointed not to see you at Mansfield Park when I called upon Lady Bertram on my return from Bath. I was concerned when she told me that you had

set out on such a long journey at such a time of year. I was the more concerned when I heard that neither of you might be returning to Mansfield Park. It is no affair of mine but it makes me anxious to think that you may be without suitable dwelling even for a while. I do not know what I can do to help you but I will write separately my address at Sotherton and of my house in town and do humbly beg you to let me know if I can provide shelter or transport or any means of relief. Please forgive my presumption. Yrs,

James Rushworth.'

'Bless the man!' cried Caroline when she had read the letter. She laughed, but not scornfully; she turned the page to see that Mr Rushworth had directed his missive to 'The Crown Inn, Skenwith, Cumberland.' 'He speaks as if Lady Bertram had flung us out upon a cruel world to starve. Can he suppose so? And who can have told him about the Crown Inn?'

'I can guess the answer to both questions,' replied Susan in a grim tone. 'He called again at Mansfield and Decima filled him up with some of her romantic stories.'

'Oh yes—I am sure that is what must have happened. I wonder that he believed her. I must write and tell him about my "quite considerable fortune", must I not. And make it clear that you are sharing in all my adventures and do not need—No, I could not reject his kindness in such a way as to make him feel unnecessary . . . It is a simple, straightforward letter and deserves more . . .'

'I suppose he is a simple straightforward man. It will be difficult to answer. And another thing: He does not say *when* he will be in either town or Sotherton, and with or without his mother. You remember that our family speak of his mother as if she dominated him? Could it be that she reads his letters? We would not like to break his confidence . . .'

The trickiness of replying to Mr Rushworth's letter, and the slight embarrassment it laid upon both Susan and Caroline, prevented a quick answer. Also it happened just now that a change had seemed to come upon their life in Skenwith: As they had been accepted by those who had known Caroline, and by the local gossips, so their social circle had expanded more widely, and they were accepted by the upper strata of Skenwith society. Mrs Chadwick, wife of the vicar of St Olaf's, waited on the ladies at the Crown, accompanied by three daughters, and invited them to the family dinner after matins next Sunday; Henry Watson brought a note from his wife inviting the ladies to drink tea and to hear her perform on her clavichord; the owner of Skenwith's best drapery promised to tell them of the even better shops in Carlisle so that they could choose their spring gowns; a Mr Pratt of the bookshop called to ask whether

Miss Blake would address the Skenwith Literary Circle on the subject of her brother? Culthorpe and Dick appeared to be finding interests and settling to country life; only Hound, who had picked a fight with the elegant spotted carriage dog of an overnight traveller, was in disgrace and tied to the water barrel in the yard, but Caroline kept him supplied with biscuits.

Another voice from their forsaken world threatened to make this phase recede into a pleasant interlude. They received a letter from Lady Bertram. Its uncharacteristic terseness of style betrayed some agitation.

She pointed out that the anniversary of Sir Thomas's death was approaching and that she felt in need of support and comfort. 'I do not know whether Julia can come. Tom must be here. He does not expect Susan. He still speaks of the Indies. How I wish we had none of these sad divisions in the family. How sad you must be in the north. I wish you had not gone.'

'So she wishes us to come back?' Susan inferred. 'I do not know what she means about Tom, but I dare not risk causing any further disharmony in the family. We must admit, Caroline, that we can be spared here now. That is, when we have dealt with Jack Barber's treasure chest—but Mr Brough can do that. We ought to go.'

'To Mansfield? But will not Tom be there . . .?'

'I think that what I shall do is to write to Julia; she invited me at one point. Supposing you were to leave me in Northampton, then I could take the London coach from there.'

'But ... Oh, yes, I suppose too that that would be a practical plan in the first place.'

'Yes; I can be very practical when necessary.'

'And one of us should certainly go to Lady Bertram. And of course to Decima, who has been away from home for so long.'

'Probably the same would be true of Culthorpe and Dick if we were to inquire.'

'I hope so. I expect Julia would let you stay in her house even were she at Mansfield. We shall meet again soon—'

'Certainly we shall. If not in our cottage with the orchard.—Oh, why are we making such a solemn business of this? Life is long and the world is wide!'

Neither prospect was at the moment particularly inviting. It may have been an illusion, that they had been so happy here. What they could not admit was that, when Mr Trotter took possession of Dunsyke they would be excluded; they would have no occasion to visit the place again.

The total reversal of the feelings with which she had undertaken the visit did not strike Caroline at the moment; she saw no future in spite of the 'considerable' fortune yielded by the house and its unexpected treasures. Nor could Susan imagine what would become of herself, self-exiled from Mansfield Park after so many happy years. Duty called; they began soberly to make preparations for their return journey.

CHAPTER SEVENTEEN

The year following the death of his father had been the most wretched of Tom's life. Heaven knew that, a year ago, he had been suffering troubles enough of his own, but his elevation had but added to them, and in all he had achieved nothing; he had been to and fro between town and country to no effect, leaving behind him in each place indecisions that caught up on him again on his return.

He had to accept Susan's refusal to marry him as a decision, on her part, but on his own it threw him into new perplexities. He was divided against himself. He resented being so much at Susan's mercy but could not help respecting her judgement. He was more and more loth to try persuasion and so was glad of her absence, yet he had been so much used to discuss with her whatever happened to be on his mind that his mind was nowadays dangerously blank. Pride, of course, still insisted that he could not make a mistake, but some form of good manners somehow inhibited the notion of saying to a lady: Very well, I do not want you, after all. One must prove oneself faithful, even if there was an occasional gleam of hope in confessing that one was not. He could admit himself unworthy but pride again denied that. Besides who would care? Not Susan. Tom was at this juncture so low-spirited that he suspected everyone of despising him. His mother depressed him; that impudent little Decima irritated him; his clerical brother preached at him; he was bereft even of the solacing company of his crony Culthorpe. He heard the stablelads calling to one another: 'Is Sir Tom hunting tomorrow, d'ye know?' No one ascribed to him the status of baronet. No one took him seriously—least of all himself. In a sense he perhaps never had; but he had never supposed that to be a form of failure.

He had forgotten the date of his father's demise, and was ashamed of that, and shamed into speaking ungraciously to his mother when she told him of her wishes; his own wishes, not to have to meet Susan, prevailed; in the event only Miss Blake returned to the Park, while Susan went on to Marylebone—at Julia's invitation, he was told; so he was banned now from that house, which most tiresome, since he had been hoping to go up to town soon.

He was not sorry to have Miss Blake again in residence. She was in no way mixed up in the family issues, she listened to Decima's chatter and was of evident comfort to his mother, and Tom himself was amused by some of her tales of the adventures in the north. He had been used to think of Miss Blake as pretty but prim, and of a negative nature because she was besotted with her brother's poetry; but now she seemed altogether more wide-awake and prettier with it. The grandfather, squirrelling away gold coins in his hovel, must have been an ogre in his time but she spoke of him tolerantly. Culthorpe's verdict was: 'Aye, they's a right brave pair of lasses, those girls.'

The atmosphere at the Park was a little lightened and Tom might the sooner get away. He came into the drawingroom one rainy morning in a lighter mood, to find Lady Bertram not yet downstairs but Miss Blake and Decima already at the table with their work, and that oaf Rushworth sitting beside them with nothing to say for himself.

'Oh . . . Rushworth; g'day to you . . .'

'I am early,' Rushworth pointed out unnecessarily, 'but the ladies were good enough to receive me. I wished to ask if they were come home.'

'Well, one of them is, as you see. Miss Price is in town, they say.'

Miss Blake took up: 'And I was just asking Decima what sort of stories she has been telling Mr Rushworth.'

'About what?' Tom wondered.

'About us. He had been alarmed to hear that

174

Susan and I were not returning here—and I do not know what else.'

'That is all I *said*,' cried Decima. 'And I said, *perhaps*—'

'Precisely. You were romancing; we guessed that.'

The sternness of her tone took Tom a little aback, and goaded Decima who said defiantly: 'Well, we all knew that Tom and Susan were not to be married and Susan had gone away—'

'But you should not have bothered Mr Rushworth about it. I think you should apologise to him.'

'I am afraid I was much concerned,' James put in, doing the apologising. No one seemed to wonder how he had heard the tale; no one to his gratitude mentioned his letter to the Crown Inn. Decima persisted:

'I suppose you think I was just romancing—'

'Yes, Decima, I do.'

'You do not *understand*. Supposing she really loves Tom? Old people, like you, have forgotten what love is.' Signor Lasso had been in Decima's mind again lately. 'And it is well for you, Caroline, now that you are a woman of large fortune and can do as you wish. While I am kept here, being called a "good girl" and blamed for being *romantic* and for being in love—'

'I think,' announced James Rushworth gravely, 'that people who are truly in love do not much talk about it.'

This statement, if a *non sequitur*, issuing from him, brought a silence, till Caroline said more gently: 'You will be going home soon, Decima; I expect your mother and father will take you with them if they come for the memorial service for Sir Thomas, and you *have* been very good to stay here, and we all think so—'

'I do not *want* to be good!' With a burst of tears Decima dashed from the room slamming the door. Tom laughed.

'She has made a fair start on her chosen course. For that exhibition I suppose she should apologise. Do *you* remember what love is, Rushworth?' James looked merely puzzled. 'By the way Miss Blake,' Tom added, 'should we congratulate you on your large fortune, or is that a part of Decima's romancing? Forgive my asking.'

'Mr Watson thinks,' Caroline told him simply, 'that when it is all settled, I shall have about six thousand pounds.'

The two gentlemen exchanged a half-glance of comment. The master of Sotherton might not have missed such a sum; the master of Mansfield Park had debts probably amounting to it. Tom remarked:

'Not, in fact, a "large" fortune.'

'To me, it is.'

She was folding away the strip of needlework which Decima had flung across the table at her stormy departure, and Tom and

176

James watched her, pensively, both becoming aware of some change in her, unable to identify it.

To James it was as if since he had last seen her she had become—Clearer? No—more real ... Human? As if his nymph—his Ondine—had been released into human form. It was strange and marvellous to him. His untrained imagination conceived an image like that of a bird, rising up in brilliant plumage into open air; his dearest wish was to set her free; but how ...?

Tom's impression was similar, if less poetic. The skirmish with Decima, the candour about money, perhaps the recollection of Culthorpe's tribute, pointed out to him that Miss Blake was indeed grown more human and approachable. At the same time she was exposed to some unprecedented risk, setting out into the world with her 'large' fortune and no protector or family; well, and must she? It was totally unprecedented that Tom employed the word that had been the bane of his life in admitting to himself: I suppose, in a way I should be responsible for her.

At this moment, Lady Bertram entered the room. 'Why is Decima sitting on the stairs crying?' she inquired. 'Oh, Mr Rushworth, good morning to you.—She cannot be so unhappy about her grandfather still?'

Probably not, but no one said so. 'I will go to her,' said Caroline, rising. Lady Bertram, settling herself on the sofa and taking up her embroidery frame, observed:

'We must all feel sad, but the mourning year is almost spent. Where is Susan?'

'She is at Julia's, ma'am.'

'Oh yes. Caroline, I am missing the purple silk . . .' But Caroline had gone. It was James Rushworth who rose to search for the silk; Tom noted: 'I suppose the man acts as lady's maid to his own mother too. It is about all he is fit for.'

If he could not have access to Julia's house, where many of the possessions from his own vacated house were stored—and if he might not in decency quit the Park before his father's memorial service—it was small wonder that Tom's temper did not improve during these wasted weeks. Nor was he mollified by Julia's manner when she and John Yates arrived on the day preceding the service.

'I assume you have left Susan alone in Marylebone,' Tom challenged her.

'Oh, no. She was with us for only a few days before she moved on to visit some friends—'

'So I could have come—What friends? Where?'

'Oh, Tom, do leave the poor girl in peace!'

This—it seemed to him, reasonably—infuriated him. 'What else have I done, for G-'s sake, for the last several months? No one can accuse me of afflicting her—'

'No, but you must let her go. Susan can take

178

care of herself.'

'I am fully assured of that, I promise you.'

Then, Julia seemed to assume, he should have nothing to complain of. In deference to the family occasion he did not mention Susan again to anyone; he let John Yates bore him with lengthy tales of the Orion Theatre and its more promising prospects; he could not believe that he himself had ever been much concerned with the place, or with theatres at all. As soon as he might, he would escape to town, put up at his club if he must, and set himself to sorting and removing the clutter in the Marylebone house; in fact why should he not stay there? Julia and John had decided to remain at Mansfield for a few days' rest; it was—as it had been, naturally, at the same time of last year—dawning spring, and Julia had had the same impulse to enjoy the season now that she had been reminded of it.

With perfunctory farewells, he travelled to a dank and unwelcoming London, bracing himself to tackle some useful chore and thereby raise his morale. After an uncomfortable night at his club he strode to Marylebone letting himself into the house with the key that he kept, leading into a side door by the conservatory. No one was about, but a shrieking of female voices from below suggested that the housemaids were quarrelling; scowling, he made a leap for the stairs and almost collided with someone as

179

rapidly descending; he and Susan halted face to face.

Recoiling, Tom cried: 'What are *you* doing here?'

As surprised as he, she held out a wisp of bright silk and said uncertainly: 'I am to send . . . Julia's Indian scarf . . .' She was in bonnet and cloak, outdoor dress. So she was not staying here? He presumed not, but passed on to the deduction:

'Julia asked you to send it to the Park? Why?—So Julia knows where you are—if it is not here?'

Apparently recovering her wits Susan smiled. 'Oh yes, Julia knows that I have been staying with the Rushworths in Wimpole Street.'

'But why should you do *that*?' He could only—wildly—guess that she was employed as lady's maid to Rushworth's mother; but her reply was more wildly incredible:

'Mr Rushworth has asked me to marry him.'

'*Pah!*'

'And I have accepted his proposal.'

'Are you quite *mad*?' Tom shouted.

'Would you think it madness, to wish to become the mistress of Sotherton?'

'Sotherton has nothing to do with it!' He inevitably knew Susan better than that. 'You cannot marry Rushworth and you know it. The man is stupid and boring and a *joke*—'

'I have never thought so.' She was now quite

calm. Rather than recede up the stairs, she circled the furious Tom and descended to the level of the hallway. Now he was above her and shouting down at her but it gave him no advantage; Susan was folding the silk scarf and putting it into her carrying bag. Reminded, Tom demanded: 'Does Julia know about this nonsense—about you and Rushworth?'

'Oh yes; she has been very generous about seeing my point of view.'

'I cannot imagine what that is. But look here—it has been too sudden. Only a couple of days ago Rushworth was at the Park, handing my mother her sewing silk—'

'It is more like a couple of weeks, Tom. He told me about it. After that, he came straight to town since his mother was here and he wished us to meet.'

'Ah yes—Rushworth's mother!' echoed Tom in a tone of some gratification. 'And how do you find that lady?'

Susan laughed. 'As you could expect, she was horrified when she discovered that I was a connection of the Bertram family. She is sure I will be like my cousin Maria and run away with the first handsome man who crosses our path, abandoning poor James. Well, I must go. We have decided, by the way, to tell no one of our engagement until after Sir Thomas's memorial service. Then we shall marry soon after Easter.' She turned towards the house door.

'No—Wait!' He was still incredulous, but

knew Susan was implacable. One could not call her obstinate, perverse, self-willed or anything so offensive, because she went about her schemes with a smooth and gentle resolution and as gentle a confidence. Tom descended the stairs to appeal to her in quiet bewilderment:

'But, Susan—I truly cannot imagine what you can *see* in the man.'

'No . . . ?' She might have pointed out that Tom's opinion of her betrothed signified nothing, but after pondering for a while she said slowly: 'I think, that when there is love, one does not reckon up the qualities that lie behind it. That comes afterwards. *Now* I know that James is . . . Kind. Trustworthy. Patient. Modest .... . I could have seen all these virtues all along but until—And I think him a fine-looking man, you know . . . Until I loved him I did not notice . . .'

But that still did not explain *how* she had come to love the man. Perhaps that was always mysterious. Tom, applying Rushworth's virtuous qualities unhopefully to himself, admitted that they were not at all applicable; but according to Susan's reasoning, why should that have prevented her from *loving* Tom?

He sighed heavily, baffled. Susan moving away was asking: 'When will you be going back to Mansfield?'

'Oh—I have not decided . . .'

'Julia in this letter,' added Susan 'says they

182

will be returning after another week or so. Bringing Decima.'

'I am glad at least of that.'

'But, Tom, it will all be easier again now, will it not: You and I need not avoid one another—indeed I cannot think why we did. We can be cousins and friends again.'

'If you wish it,' he replied with a gloom which concealed a gleam of light. Yes, it might be a relief—and correct—to cease acting the rejected suitor.

'Oh, and Tom,' proceeded Susan in her normal brisk voice. 'I shall probably be at Wimpole Street now until the time of the wedding. When you are at Mansfield I do wish you would look after Caroline a little, especially if she receives letters from Dunsyke about the sale of the house, and needs advice.—And do not allow Aunt Bertram to keep her always indoors now the spring is coming.'

'Very well,' agreed Tom, absently. He was still dumbfounded by this encounter and situation but as he started on the chore of tidying his books to be packed for Mansfield he did begin to feel that something might be retrieved from the confusion. Why, he now wondered in passing, had Rushworth come to *love* Susan? All the virtues were on her side and was Rushworth capable of love? Heaven knew; and what ill chance blighted Tom, to have the same dull and useless brother-in-law inflicted upon him *twice* in his life?

CHAPTER EIGHTEEN

The news that had so astounded Tom was received by the others of the family with only a mild surprise; it was not that it had been expected; just it came about so naturally; everyone save for Tom and Mrs Rushworth was pleased. Decima, of course, deplored the absence of passionate excitement; she could not place any value on simple affection, deeply as it was now revealed in the happy lovers.

For Susan, her James must have been the husband she had unawarely conceived of, years ago: The calm, understanding, steadfast man to be preferred to her dashing cousin Tom. And Tom—among others—well might be puzzled to explain the workings in James Rushworth's mind regarding love. James himself could not have explained it; how could his painful adoration of his water-nymph have cleared his heart for the exquisite, comforting love of Susan? He had thought that she was attached to her cousin Tom, and her rejection of him had given James a daring hope; when she accepted his proposal James's own confidence surprised him.

When Tom called at Wimpole Street, to discuss arrangements for the wedding, an

184

occasion that he expected to be hideous was made tolerable by Rushworth's being unusually articulate; he and Susan had everything planned in total agreement. Susan wished to be married from Mansfield Park, with her cousin Edmund officiating. Her brother William the Rear Admiral was coming up to give her away; then they and he would travel down to Portsmouth so that Mrs Price could meet her new son-in-law; after which they would return to Sotherton for the summer, taking Caroline with them for a visit.

This part of the plan somehow displeased Tom. 'Well, Rushworth, do not you elope with Caroline. That would kill your mother outright.'

'I dare say it would,' said James, easily laughing. 'My mother is ready to expect disaster in everything. But she will not fail to accept Susan; how could she! Indeed she loves her already.'

The wedding was to take place at Whitsuntide; meanwhile Julia was to help Susan buy her wedding clothes; as he was about to leave, Tom was struck by a thought: 'But Susan, have you any money?'

'Oh, yes, your solicitors have been sending me my allowance; you must remember to stop that.'

Here was Susan directing his affairs as usual. Mrs James Rushworth would never be short of money, but it was incorrect to have the bridegroom buy the wedding clothes, Tom was pretty sure; Rushworth had the tact to say nothing; Tom groaned inwardly at the recollection of all the work he must take upon himself in the permanent absence of Susan. He would have to admit, however, to himself and others, that Susan and her James appeared perfectly happy.

He admitted it bravely, when he returned to the Park, to his mother and to Caroline. Here, the scene was more cheerful than it had been for some time; the cuckoo sang, blossom scented the air, and the shadows of mourning were past; Lady Bertram was looking forward so eagerly to the wedding and to wearing her new rose-pink gown that she did not look beyond that or complain that she missed Susan; for Caroline was with her, was she not? And as attentive as ever.

Tom observed this with some misgiving. What could Susan have meant by asking him to 'look after' Caroline? She appeared contented enough, but he could not shake off the notion that she ought not to be, nor ought she to remain an appendage of the Bertram family. She too was looking forward to the wedding— at which she was to be Susan's attendant, also in a new gown—but, after that? He asked her suddenly one day as she was walking with the pugs on the terrace, and was dismayed to hear for the first time about the cottage in Dunsyke village and its apple trees.

'You cannot mean that seriously!' he exclaimed. She did not insist or invite any protest; he had another pang of misgiving, but forbore to express it.

Then one day as he came in from the stables she called to him across the lobby: 'Tom! Have you a moment, please—I have had a letter from Mr Yates that I would like to show you—'

Now why did he feel a prick of satisfaction because he had been promoted to his Christian name while John Yates was still 'Mr'? He sat with the letter on a windowsill and she sat beside him. 'Oh, excellent!' he said, reading. The secretary of the great Josiah Willett had evidently dug through to the doormat and found 'The Death of Wisdom' and thought it worth the great man's perusal; he mentioned however that *if* the play were to be put into production, a minimum of twenty printed copies must be supplied.

'I see the force of that,' Caroline conceded. 'Mr Willett has not yet even seen it, has he, though; I suppose I could find a printer in Northampton who would make the copies; would it be worth it?'

'It is a gamble to be taken,' Tom advised her. 'You would do better to spend your six thousand pounds on that, rather than on cottages in the far north of the country.'

'Of course, I had forgotten . . .' If she could forget her large fortune, could it be important to her? She was going on:

187

'There was another thing: I told you I think about Mr Trotter, and his purchasing a whole fresh edition of Stephen's poems—only to raise the tone of his house—almost as a decoration—I do not know that he reads poetry himself—Do you think that can be right?'

'My dear, you must not set your principles too high. Mr Trotter said he was intending to give away copies—but to whom? All his friends may not be as semi-literate as he. I like the sound of Mr Trotter and I am sure your brother would, and would be grateful for any dissemination of his works.'

'Yes. Of course. Thank you . . . I am glad I asked you.'

'I am going into Northampton tomorrow. Give me a copy of that play and I will find a printer.' He felt surprisingly pleased with himself. But on the next morning when Culthorpe remarked to him: 'Weddings are in the air,' Tom flinched. Why? Culthorpe merely went on to say: 'My sister's son Dick is taking up with Nancy from the smithy . . .'

Tom wished for Dick the greatest of wedded bliss, but from long habit shied away from such a thing for himself. He was, all the same, aware of a peculiar and peaceful happiness in this quiet Paschaltide with the halcyon weather and a sense of lull before the wedding—And, with Caroline's company. Mindful of Susan's commands he took Caroline out riding frequently. Demoiselle the roan mare had strained a hock and Culthorpe had kept her out to grass to rest, so Caroline rode a sturdy dun pony whose general duties included pulling a mowing machine on the lawns, but who trotted along proudly under her. As they passed the paddock one morning Tom shook his head:

'I wish Culthorpe would bring that beast in before she blows herself out on all this new grass. I had rather you rode her—'

'I am quite happy with old Titus; he reminds me of a fell pony.'

'His paces are not good. You will notice the difference when you mount Demoiselle again. She will suit you well.'

'Yes, but she must go to Sotherton. You gave her to Susan, did you not?'

'I suppose I did,' agreed Tom, ungraciously. '—Yes of course I did.' He decided to tell Culthorpe to ask about for a steed as good as Demoiselle to be given to Caroline, forgetful that she might ride away on it to her northern wastes. He could not contemplate her leaving Mansfield: what could he do to detain her here?

He was in a way of detaining himself, yielding to the holiday spirit of this interlude. After the wedding, he would apply himself again to estate business; there was no need to worry at present.

One member of the wedding party could not

189

have less echoed the sentiment: Poor Mrs Rushworth was worried very nearly out of her wits. In the Wimpole Street house she happened to overhear James chatting and laughing with this pleasant, charming, well-mannered, handsome, amusing girl—as if he had not a care in the world; this was dangerous for him but he did not see it; nor, in effect, did his mother and this perplexed her. Mrs Rushworth was falling into the self-contrived trap of the compulsive worrier: A thing is too good to be true; *ergo* it is untrue; but if the falsity is imperceptible—where does truth lie? Mrs Rushworth retreated into total confusion. Some days before the wedding she announced that she must spend more time in solitude at Sotherton, whence she was to attend the wedding, for peace and reflection.

Neither did she achieve. Alone, she was the more distraught. On the day after her arrival she felt desperately that she must speak to— confide in—appeal to—someone; early, she sent for her carriage and was driven to Mansfield Park. Surely Lady Bertram—a mother herself—would sympathise and support her. In what, Mrs Rushworth did not foresee—Could Lady Bertram stop the wedding? Mrs Rushworth had an unformed intention of flinging herself on Lady Bertram's mercy, and was unprepared for the spectacle of that lady as she found her.

On this balmy morning Lady Bertram was

sitting out of doors, in an arbour starry with clematis blossom, her embroidery frame in hand and the pugs snoring at her feet. She received Mrs Rushworth with no surprise, begging her only to take a place beside her in the shade. '. . . Please do not stand there in the sun, Mrs Rushworth. I declare it is hot enough to give one the headache. How kind of you to call.' She added to the escorting manservant: 'Please bring some wine for Mrs Rushworth . . .' and resumed her stitching with some further comment on the weather to which Mrs Rushworth's pent-up emotions could not provide a suitable reply. Instead she stared at Lady Bertram—whom she had not met for many years—in wonder; here was no frenzy to match her own; even in frenzy Mrs Rushworth recognised that Lady Bertram was no one to be confided in, affable though she was. In spite of herself, Mrs Rushworth's frenzy began to abate as she thought: But she must be of my age at least. How can her face be so smooth? How can she have lived such an untroubled life? I know that she was widowed, only last year; and that she has had worries over her family—That scandalous adulterous daughter and the other one who eloped—And they say her elder son is irresponsible . . . Does it not affect her?

It was inconceivable to her that anyone should escape the agonies of anxiety that she herself had always suffered. Yet Lady

Bertram's countenance, and temperament, bore no traces of sorrows and fears that had in their time affected her severely enough. Her resilience was admirable but easy to her, since her ordinary life had been always so untroubled. It was with a hint of uncertainty that Mrs Rushworth began:

'I felt I must speak to you—about this wedding—'

'Yes? I am so much looking forward to it.' And as Mrs Rushworth, checked in her outpouring, hesitated, she added: 'I am to have a gown of a lilac colour, with ribbons of the same tint.'

'But how *can* you?' cried Mrs Rushworth, meaning: look forward to the wedding; Lady Bertram, quite amiably seeing no reason for Mrs Rushworth to criticise her taste in gowns, was silent. Mrs Rushworth tried again:

'As a mother yourself—with such ... children, you must feel ...' She was checked again, perhaps fortunately, by an attack of simple politeness: She recollected that it was Lady Bertram's own children whom she had come to complain of. Why had she not thought of that when she set out on this ill-considered visit? What would Lady Bertram *think* of her? Apparently, nothing; she stitched on placidly while Mrs Rushworth saw herself as scrawny, elderly, and bad-tempered in contrast, and now remarked:

'I think the roses will do well this year. The

buds are showing already.'

Lady Bertram might have been mildly interested, and pleased to know that merely by her natural inertia she had soothed this fidgety lady's nerves and probably averted an emotional collapse. Mrs Rushworth was silenced, and began to feel not ungrateful for that. When she rose to leave she murmured: 'It was just that—you see—I was so worried—'

'Oh, I am sure you need not worry,' said Lady Bertram, inattentive; but Mrs Rushworth was almost tempted to believe her.

CHAPTER NINETEEN

After this encounter Mrs Rushworth was able to recognise that very soon the wedding would be over, and that she might then return to her pleasant house in Bath, which now appeared to her like the refuge she had never allowed it to be. She would have to resign James to the care of Miss Price—or, as she must now be called, Susan—and as James was so smiling and contented, that roused no great anxiety. Mrs Rushworth's mood of calm held during the wedding celebrations; she had even sent hurriedly to Northampton for the materials for a bonnet of more festive style with yellow ribbons and flowers, though she could not flatter herself that she looked anywhere as young and pretty as Lady Bertram in a delicate shade of lilac.

Smiles and contentment and elegant garb flavoured the whole occasion. William Price was particularly struck by the beauty of the bride's attendant, the 'Caroline' of whom his sister had so often written in her letters. 'Lovely girl, that!' he nudged his cousin Tom in his bluff nautical manner; but Tom's agreement was indicated in so tight-lipped a fashion that William said to himself: 'Oho! Is that how the wind blows—Is Tom to be shackled at last?' and altered his own manner tactfully, becoming serious:

'Look ye here, Tom, while I see you, I want to speak about the estates in Jamaica. I was in the Indies last year and some friends of mine are just returned from there. What have you arranged about it all?'

'. . . All what?' asked Tom, conscious that he sounded guilty—which he was; he hated the thought of those phalanxes of mouldering sugar cane—but unable to evade William's directness.

'The whole venture, I dare say it was a sound investment in your grandfather's day, but what is it bringing in now?'

'. . . I am not closely in touch—'

'Nothing, I'll wager.' And William described the state of Jamaica as he and his fellow mariners had observed it: the shortage of labour and the Creoles who now absorbed what there was; the constant storms; the niggardliness of the insurance companies; the useless outlay in introducing a new crop;—'My advice is, sell up.'

'My father thought of doing so, but could not get his price—'

'Sell at a loss, then, and be quit. Anyone will buy anything if the price is low enough. What sort of a manager have you out there?'

'Stevenson—my father's steward and factor, whom my father sent out there about . . . five years ago? He's a capable man but as you can suppose, not happy in the situation.' Indeed the letters Tom had been receiving from Stevenson contained such dire plaints that Tom had been unequal to answering them. Therein lay the burden of his guilt over the Indies problem. William said:

'Then I suggest that you order the capable Stevenson to sell up the whole parcel, and bring him home to take up his old job. You should find him useful now that you have lost Susan.'

Tom wondered that he himself had not conceived such a brilliant idea. He had liked Stevenson and was already missing Susan in his work. To be rid of those plantations too would be a huge relief, cost what it might; he would think of other economies to offset it; or surely Stevenson would.

Thus encouraged, Tom announced William's plan to Julia and John Yates at their dinner table some two weeks after the wedding, when he had occasion to spend a few days in town and had, as erstwhile, favoured them with his company. He was taken aback when Julia said:

'But, Tom, why did you need William to think of this? Is it not time that you took some decisions yourself about the estate—?'

'My dear Julia, you must know how much I have put myself about during this whole year, to care for the whole estate as our father would have wished—'

'Taradiddle. He would not have wished you to lose his valuable overseas properties, for an instance.'

'Now, my dear,' protested John Yates, 'we know that Tom has had so many new responsibilities lately, and that, considering everything, he has coped with them pretty well.'

Considering what? Tom wondered; considering Tom's laziness and ineptitude? It was well for John Yates, optimistic now that the Orion Theatre was fairly launched; he was full of energy and had, after reading a printed copy of 'The Death of Wisdom', admired it. He meant to employ the texts, instead of committing them yet to Josiah Willett's doormat, by producing a public reading of the drama and was recruiting a cast with enthusiasm. 'I was thinking,' he now added to Tom, 'of having Peter March to read the part of Cebes. His voice has the suitable tone—'

'Yes, yes. I wish you all success. But, about those plantations—'

'We must remember,' said Decima in the gracious grown-up manner she had of late cultivated, 'that Uncle Tom has not had a happy year, apart from the worry of the estates.'

Tom stared at her. Grown-up or not, her impudence persisted. Her mother said: 'That does not concern you, Decima.'

'Oh but it does, Mama. And I for one am glad that Susan is so happy.'

That was disregarded. Julia changed the subject: 'I hope Caroline will be able to come to town and hear the play reading. When is she to pay her visit to Sotherton, Tom? Do you know?'

'I suppose, as soon as the happy pair return from Portsmouth.'

'And for how long will she stay there?'

'That I have not been told.'

Decima contributed: 'She may stay there to live, you know.'

'I did *not* know,' Tom's voice was like the crack of a whip. 'Who told you that?'

'Why—She did. Caroline. On the day of the wedding. We were talking, and she said how lucky Susan was to go to such a beautiful place as Sotherton, and how lucky she was to have a friend—You know, it is a good idea—Do you not think so? Caroline and Susan have agreed so well together, and Susan might need company, apart from that dull old James—'

'Decima!' John Yates intervened severely. 'Mr Rushworth is now related to you by marriage and becomes a member of our family. You will please speak of him with respect.'

'Yes, very well.—Caroline said she and Susan were thinking of sharing a cottage in Cumberland, but that Sotherton was a far more pleasant place to live, and I am sure she is right.'

Tom was persuaded of nothing of the kind. The shock of Decima's announcement brought the more vividly to his mind the intention— now shattered—of his marrying Caroline: it was as painful to him as if he had already proposed and been rejected; how could he lose her to the bosky glades of beautiful Sotherton? She had surely understood, during the halcyon interlude before the wedding, that Tom loved her? Decima was chattering on:

'. . . And you see, my relative-by-marriage still has the house in Wimpole Street, does he not, and they will be coming up to town, all of them, so we shall see them often. And I am glad, because you know Caroline was *my* friend first and I love her—'

'So do we all. She is in effect a member of the family and you need not claim possession of her,' said Julia. Tom flinched. Did he come late in the claimants to Caroline? That was dismissal indeed. As if from an outer darkness he voiced an impulse of despair:

'Well then, Julia, if you think I have failed in all my duties, I may as well go myself to Antigua and see what I can do to redeem myself...'

No one took that too seriously; Julia was accustomed to her brother's self-dramatisation under reproof, though she did not see why he had flashed up so, at that point in the conversation. She too remembered Stevenson and judged him every bit as capable as Tom in the disposal of the unlucky plantations. 'It need not come to that,' she comforted Tom kindly, but little to his comfort.

It was Decima who, reminded of her affection for her friend Caroline, decided to write to her although as usual there was nothing much to say: '... My satin dancing pumps are too tight but my feet cannot still be growing? I do not look forward to the ball or to anything else in this dreary town. I am still determined to become an actress. My Uncle Tom is still with us but I do not know why or for how long. He is out of temper and is going to the Indies. I do not know what good he can do there. I have spent all my allowance on a bright green cape and it matches nothing else, least of all my complexion...'

The part of these tidings most disturbing to Caroline is easily guessed. The defection of Tom to the Indies struck her as cruelly as her

199

defection to Sotherton had struck Tom; both were too much amazed to allow for Tom's impetuousness or Decima's exaggeration. Both felt a disappointment unjustified by the circumstances: After all, they had not been betrothed; only now did they feel the loss of an accord that had grown upon them naturally in their summertime closeness. Even now, Caroline could not admit to herself: But I love him! But she did. In many ways she had valued and admired him and may have entertained, distantly, the thought: Why can Susan not marry him? *I* could ... It was simply not possible that Tom should entertain aspirations towards marriage for two women in such rapid succession; for that reason alone Caroline had herself denied any such aspirations; she could not deduce that, in Tom's complicated emotions, his love for Susan and for herself were aspects of the same process. All she was now conscious of was a sudden gulf in her whole life, an absence of Tom. At the least he could have warned her of his projected departure? Was she so negligible to him? He was evidently of unsuspected importance to herself.

So she pined and fretted and kept up a calm manner before Lady Bertram, only informing her: 'Tom is thinking of going to the Indies himself, ma'am, to look into affairs there.'

'Yes; he went before, you know, with his father, and they brought me some brightly-coloured shawls—No, now I remember, they brought me a necklace of jade; it was William, your brother, who gave me the shawls, when he went to the Indies as a young officer.—No, I am confused—I confuse you with Susan!' She shook her head at herself. 'But now Susan is married and I must make the best of it. I am so fortunate to have you with me still, Caroline.'

'I am glad to be with you, ma'am.'

'But if you go to live in Cumberland,' went on Lady Bertram after more reflection, 'I shall be truly alone. I do not know what I shall do.'

'It may not come to that,' Caroline said, to offer the unreasoning hope that usually mollified Lady Bertram for as long as her plaints lasted. But indeed Caroline's own plaints had become more grievous; she thought wistfully of the cottage at Dunsyke; she herself was again, and wretchedly, alone in the world. Mr Piper wrote to her telling of the operations of Mr Trotter, who was carrying out a great tree-planting scheme in the region of the house, and building a new stable block, and was well satisfied by his new property.

'I cannot believe,' Lady Bertram took up after another pause, 'that you could be happy at all, living so far away, among all those strange people. I am sure it is time for my tea—Would you ring for the tea things, my dear?'

Caroline could have been happy at Mansfield Park, even as a surrogate Susan, had it not been for the absence—and the threat of the presence—of Tom, who seemed to be lingering in town, unaccountably; what had he to do there just now?

Tom could have told her: Nothing. He was hoping to stay away until Caroline had made her removal to Sotherton (which, need it be said, was not at all her intention; her remarks to Decima on the subject had been merely hypothetical.) Nor had her remarks to Lady Bertram about Dunsyke had any practical application; it was not surprising that her ladyship dismissed that project so easily.

'I wish Tom need not be so long away,' Lady Bertram said as Caroline made the tea. 'You do not suppose he is off to the Indies without coming home first? He cannot have heard yet from Stevenson. That will take several weeks; he will have to be patient.'

That advice could have been extended to others besides Tom. Julia for one was becoming exasperated. There was a feeling between herself and William but gaining in acceptance, that Tom loved Caroline. Then, why did he do nothing about it? There was no hindrance; the family loved her; why was he hanging about in Marylebone, irritable and gloomy? But Tom in love was his own creature; Tom unhappy was unapproachable, which added to Julia's annoyance. She heartily wished that he would declare himself to Caroline or go to the Indies, if not both; in private she expressed these views to John and to Decima; John said:

'Lord, yes, she is just the girl for him if only he would see it.'

Tom saw it. He admired and was passionately drawn to Caroline. His personal hindrance was the obdurate and life-long prejudice he had against marriage as such—in the abstract. The abstraction was formed from the marriages he had observed among his friends—so often, marriage meant assuming responsibility, acquiring a dependant however loving; this repugnance came into collision with his positive feeling; he was at a loss. Unwillingly, he may have taken note of his own mother, to whose wishes his father had always been obedient; about this, he was ashamed of his disloyalty, and might have been a little fortified had he known that his niece Decima saw the drawback to Caroline's marrying Tom; It might consign her to a lifetime's attendance on Decima's grandmother. Decima did not point out the likelihood to anyone, least of all to her uncle, with whom no discussion was permissible, but she was apprehensive for Caroline, who would find no way out of the difficulty.

It did not occur to Tom that he was so much pleased to be able to help and advise Caroline when the opportunity arose; that he had in practice delighted in her dependence just as he had appreciated Susan's being able to 'take care of herself'; but prejudice does not yield to the rational.

The situation was slightly relieved by the arrival in Marylebone for dinner one day of Mr and Mrs James Rushworth—a much-travelled pair; they had, since their wedding, paid their visit to Portsmouth, then to recuperate from that (as they freely admitted) had spent a holiday week in Bournemouth before going on to Bath to visit Mrs Rushworth; now they were in Wimpole Street for a few days on their way home to Sotherton.

'So we should be home by the seventeenth of the month,' Susan said at the dinner table. 'I have written to Caroline suggesting that she come about a week after that; I feel I shall need a little time to unpack and settle in.' It did not escape Tom that she spoke of Sotherton as 'home', although she could have spent only a day and a half of her life there, between her wedding and the subsequent travels. Little did escape him as he sat stony-faced amid the family's conviviality; he had not even the spirit to feel any envy of Rushworth, who was so placidly at ease. It was only at the mention of Caroline's name that Tom stirred:

'I understand that she is coming to live at Sotherton?'

'—Caroline is? I have heard nothing of that,' said Susan in surprise. 'Who told you—?'

'Decima did.'

'*I?* Well, that is what I understood Caroline

204

to say,' Decima confessed. '—Or did I misunderstand...' she quavered under Tom's stern glance.

'She would be very welcome,' Rushworth said.

'Of course. But I hardly suppose she would invite herself without consulting me or James.'

'No—I am sure she did not mean... And Grandmama cannot spare her...' Decima persisted, drawing a darker glance from Tom, who was now afraid he had merely made himself look foolish, to have taken Decima's miscitation seriously. He decided that at the least he would now return to the Park, before Caroline left for her visit to Sotherton, if only to escape the attentions of his solicitous womenfolk here. When the guests had left he went upstairs to sort out the possessions from his rented house that were still piled along the passage outside his room—relics of a lost life, they might have been; books, sheet music, opera cloaks, dancing shoes—urban trivialities. To him arrived Decima, who sat with folded hands, offering help, but more intent on a display of the womanly wisdom and sympathy that was among her current rôles.

'I'm sorry if I offended you about Caroline. You must not feel I do not understand. It is important to me—'

'It is important to *me* to tidy up some of this clutter—'

'Yes; the servants are complaining. I was

thinking, you know, how much Caroline has changed since we knew her. You remember how thin she was, and her wornout clothes, and she thought of nothing but sewing—'

'I cannot say I remember.'

'But now she could be—anyone. It would be a pity for her to go and live by herself in a cottage, do you not agree? She deserves much more than that. But in a way she is still ... humble. I am so fond of her.'

'Would you have any use for the Poems of Spenser?' asked Tom, clapping the dust out of them.

Decima opened her mouth to say that Caroline might, but forbore. 'I do in general think,' she pronounced, 'that people *should* be married. Consider Mr Rushworth—my new Uncle James. He is not at all foolish or dull now that he has Susan. No one could laugh at him.'

'If I take your implication,' said Tom shaking out a silver-frogged evening cape, 'you recommend me too to marry. I thank you for your concern, and hope you would find me laughable if I proved to be a confirmed bachelor.'

'Oh, but I am sure you are not,' said Decima, as gently persuasive as if he had accused himself of some base and shameful offence. 'And, Uncle Tom, *I* would never laugh at you!'

He received this reassurance with no
206

evident gratitude.

CHAPTER TWENTY

Tom, returning to Mansfield Park after an absence, never gave warning; this was 'home' and formalities unnecessary. Caroline was prepared to be unprepared, but this time she felt a sharper pang than usual when he walked into the drawingroom; was it of relief that he was not gone to the Indies, or of anxiety that he looked so stern and preoccupied? It soon appeared that he had come across a new obstacle to the domestic solvency of the household: The number of servants, many of them useless. The place was over-staffed and silted up with wage-earners who had ceased to justify the wages but drifted along in semi-obscurity—

'... Like that old nitwit we call the "librarian"—Susan and I put him in the office and gave him old ledgers to play with—just to keep him occupied. Meanwhile the library is neglected and we do need to have it catalogued and weeded out; it is in a disgraceful state. And how many dotards are hanging about the back offices, I hate to imagine; the books have barely been kept. There is always some unexplained veteran sitting in a corner or on a doorstep holding a duster and half asleep—'

All this he declared to his mother, who replied calmly: 'Yes, it is difficult to know what to do with servants when they are too old for their work. But Sir Thomas was so kind; he would never turn one away.'

'That is becoming evident, and it must be dealt with.'

'But they like to feel useful. Chapman still does some of my mending.'

Chapman, Lady Bertram's maid for many years, was by now bedridden and too blind for fine sewing, but the fiction persisted.

'I do not intend to be unkind, ma'am, but I am sure neither you nor my father would wish me to run the place wastefully when it is already in such straits.'

'Sir Thomas used to think it was you who wasted money,' Lady Bertram observed, placidly.

Caroline glanced up from her book to note his reaction to that; a spasm of black annoyance stiffened his face but he rejoined only:

'That will be checked by my having none to waste.'

Caroline found his mood strange altogether. He was unsmiling and civil, inattentive and busy-minded. She wondered what could have happened while he was in town, to harass him. She did not for a moment suppose it could have anything to do with herself, but was sad that their previous friendship seemed to have cooled.

Tom could have told her that, to the contrary, their friendship was in danger of boiling over and that he was in great pains to prevent that. He was so unaccustomed to inner conflict and so much puzzled by it that he found himself avoiding Caroline about the house and gardens; he was incurious about her own feelings; self-absorption enclosed him; what he needed was a shock strong enough to break him out of it, and indeed what he deserved; by chance, he received one, through no merit of his own, and not until the very day of her departure for Sotherton.

On the last day she spent at Mansfield Tom had ridden out early—to avoid her?—on a visit to the grain merchant's, and when he came back to the stable yard, there Caroline was, in conference with Culthorpe. She hailed him:

'Oh, Tom—Culthorpe says Demoiselle is quite fit again—'

'I am glad to hear it,' said Tom, dismounting.

'So, you see; I thought I might ride her over to Sotherton tomorrow.'

'Why?'

'Because, you see, Susan will want her there. She's hers.'

'Oh—I suppose so . . .'

Culthorpe spoke up: 'The mare's as sound as a bell, Sir Tom. I've had her round the Park

209

a couple of times myself. Happen she's a bit fat and frisky still from being laid off—'

'Is she?' queried Tom, sharply, turning to Caroline and saying the very thing he did not intend to: 'Then I had better ride over there with you—'

'*Will* you?' cried Caroline, smiling radiantly, but marring the effect by adding: 'Susan and James will be so glad to see you!'

'H'm.' That had been a stupid suggestion of his; he could just as well have sent a groom with her.

Culthorpe had it all arranged. 'We can soon send Miss Blake's boxes round to Sotherton by road, in the trap. It will be a fine ride for you both, through the woods. And you'll be riding Harrier again? I'll see to that hind shoe.' He patted the neck of the chestnut gelding from which Tom had dismounted, and, bustling, led it away. Tom and Caroline, left together in the sunny yard, looked at one another with an involuntary complicity. They might have declared a truce; they had always been happy riding together. And on the next morning they set out in good heart, delayed only while Lady Bertram wrote a letter which they must deliver to Susan. The morning was fine and the country in full summer; the roses that had been in bud for Susan's wedding were already scattering their petals; the dandelions were puffed away and the shade of the woods was heavy with darkness; on invisible threads, little maggots like jade carvings slowly twirled.

The riders' way led first across Mansfield Common, with its open ground and weedy ponds. Demoiselle trotted along, pretty as a porcelain pony; Caroline and Tom, still in accord, talked for no reason about the Orion Theatre and the use it might make of 'The Death of Wisdom'; at any rate, those printed copies should help to preserve it, were it staged or not. 'You would be miraculously lucky to find anyone like your Mr Trotter,' Tom remarked.

'I could not expect that. I would like to thank him—I wish I could make another visit to Dunsyke—'

'How long are you to stay at Sotherton?' Tom asked, abruptly.

'I have not been told; perhaps—a few weeks . . .?'

And then . . .? He dared not ask. She was a free spirit, with her six thousand pounds and the cottage at Dunsyke. To mention that would bring them off neutral ground. But now, they were approaching the first of the woods; Tom led the way down a steep track and across a ford. Alongside again, they cantered slowly up rising ground and need only cross another tract of common before reaching the first plantations of the Sotherton demesne. It had seemed a short journey; in a couple of miles they would be at its end. 'I had no idea that Sotherton was so close!' Caroline exclaimed when Tom said so.

'We call it ten miles by road, but we have taken some short cuts.' He thought he heard her sigh. 'As it is,' he added, 'we shall enter the grounds by a shorter side avenue; I had forgotten that you had not yet seen the place. You will find it impressive, I promise you. Now,' as they forded another stream and faced a narrow uphill path, 'do you lead the way this time; and wait at the top of the rise so that I can check the girths.'

Caroline set Demoiselle in a slow canter against the gradual slope. The path was here narrow again and bordered with clumps of bramble and wild rose. Tom followed, restraining Harrier's pace to suit hers.

And then; everything happened at once.

Out of the clustering trees burst a young stray bullock, snorting. Demoiselle shied, so violently that Caroline was flung from the saddle. As the mare swerved, Caroline lost the support of the saddle horn but her foot was caught in the stirrup. She was dragged along the ground, through the thorns and brambles, helpless as the frightened Demoiselle gained speed. Tom saw at once that the girth had slipped but had no time to reflect on it. All in the same moment he had thrashed Harrier (who was also afraid of the bullock) forward between Demoiselle and the bullock, to whom in passing he gave a slash of the whip which sent it plunging back, bellowing, into the trees;

meanwhile Tom reached forward and seized Demoiselle's bridle and hurled himself on to the ground; for an interval he was dragging at a prancing horse with each hand, still unable to see what had become of Caroline. Releasing the horses—who must look after themselves— he dived under Demoiselle's neck and snatched Caroline's foot free of the stirrup. She fell at his feet, her veil torn off and blood from the thorns streaming down her face. Her eyes were closed and he dared not guess at her injuries—surely an arm—both arms—had been broken? He knelt beside her, terrified, lifting one of her hands. When she opened her eyes and smiled at him he gathered her up recklessly, bodily, and clutched her tightly.

'I am not hurt,' she said. 'It was just that Demoiselle shied—Where is she?'

'Here. Waiting for you.'

'She is all right?'

'Yes, yes.' It was now that the shock struck him. The accident had come about 'just' because Tom had not tightened the mare's girth. He had been responsible. He had ridden with Caroline to take care of her; any fool of a stable boy would have done better. Here was the creature he had longed to cherish, and here was a far too vivid example of what can come about if one shirks responsibility. It was as if a new inner eye opened. Tom was awake.

The woods were very quiet; distantly pigeons called their soothing *'roo-roo'*; Harrier and Demoiselle were cropping the grass of the path. Tom said with fervour, as if taking an oath:

'As long as I live, I will never again see you mounted without testing the girth *myself*.'

(To anticipate: His children commented on this little foible of Papa's, and were amused, ascribing to it no great significance.)

Now Tom recognised that he and Caroline were clasped together as if sinking in a stormy sea. He released her and she sat upright, flexing her arms, touching her face and looking amazed at the blood. 'Those cruel thorns! I am glad I got none on my eye—'

'Come, we have not far to go. Let us see if you can stand—'

'Oh, yes, I can. Will you mount me?'

He demurred, but felt she might be easier riding, if he were to walk, leading both horses at a slow pace, in case of any more errant livestock. So he lifted her into the saddle, tightened the girth and draped her skirt, and then in a humble and earnest tone asked her to marry him.

Caroline must have been beyond astonishment, and shaken by her fall; she could never remember afterwards what she replied; to reply was unnecessary; all at once Tom and she were alone in the world, in a woodland glade spangled with sun; where they were supposed to be going, she had forgotten; he was dipping a kerchief into a stream and gently

214

patting her face, where the scratches were already drying; he was kissing her hand where a bramble had torn it; the moment was timeless. Tom, too, was suspended in this blissful renewal of life. It was he who finally recollected their whereabouts and purpose. He must deliver her to Sotherton, where her injuries could be attended to; one of her wrists, he had noticed, was swelling ominously. As he looked about, he seemed to remember from long ago visits that, by cutting through some shrubberies ahead, they might emerge before the main façade of the house, which he would like Caroline to see as a first impression. It was worth seeing. He wanted to give Caroline all the beauty of the world.

'I am so glad Demoiselle was not hurt,' Caroline was saying. 'We are bringing her to Susan safely.'

Susan, impatient but not yet anxious, was waiting under the colonnade of the great front door which stood open to the summer air, expecting her visitors to approach down the main avenue, expecting Caroline and Demoiselle and some escort, but puzzled to see Tom, on foot, and Caroline tattered and dusty, emerging from the direction of the knot garden; she ran to meet them, calling:

'What has happened? You are late. What is wrong?'

'Everything is *right*. We are to be married,' said Tom. 'But Caroline had a fall and must be

215

looked to—'

Delight and distress mingled in Susan as Tom lifted Caroline down. Embracing her Susan cried: 'Oh, my dear, your *face*—But that is wonderful—And your hand is hurt—I am so happy—Dear Tom, this is exactly what I wished for you—Come, Caroline, I will take you up to your room at once . . .' Turning to the various attendants who were hovering she called: 'Collins, would you take the horses—'

Caroline wished to say something about the magnificence of the house, which had certainly impressed her, but she was so grateful to be indoors in the shade that she could not find words; it was all she could do to climb the stairs. Susan was saying: 'Phillips—my maid—has your boxes unpacked already—' And from the curve of the great staircase she called again: 'Jackson, I think Sir Thomas would like a little brandy—'

Sir Thomas was in agreement. The events of the journey were less exhausting than the emotional crisis through which he had so rapidly passed; he was bewildered; he sat down on the steps and pushed his hat to the back of his head. All he could think of was that he wished he could take off his riding boots after walking over a mile and a half in them. Someone put a glass in his hand and he took it without acknowledgement; a sip of the brandy revived him but made him at the same time sleepy. It was blissful to be out of the sun, and quiet.

At this point James Rushworth appeared. He had heard sounds of arrival: Was this Miss Blake at last? The servant he inquired of told him that Sir Thomas Bertram was here, with a lady, and James was conscious of the honour. No Bertram had visited Sotherton for years. He threw down the gun he had been cleaning. The man added that Sir Thomas was at the door, and James hastened to invite him more properly into the house. When he found his distinguished guest sprawled on the steps with his hat askew, breathing fumes of spirits, he was a little disconcerted, but sizing up the situation in his own practical fashion he bent like a lackey to jack off Bertram's boots.

Tom thought dreamily: Good man, Rushworth is. He has a grasp of essentials.

CHAPTER TWENTY-ONE

The arrival of the guests had been so informal that there could be no ceremony about the rest of the day. Besides, there was far too much to explain and marvel at and recall: talk flowed as they gathered for a splendid collation including fruits from the Sotherton hothouses. Caroline was at the table, insisting that she was perfectly well, her face salved and her wrist bandaged; she could not bear to lose a minute of Tom's presence, and he had said that he must not stay here for the night: 'No, no—it is moonlight and I can keep to the road; I shall be home with no trouble.' Already he was wearing slippers of Rushworth's and was looking forward to the ride in the night air that might help him to rally his thoughts, which were in understandable disorder, the more as he could not keep his eyes away from Caroline.

'But you must visit us again—often,' Susan urged him.

James Rushworth too gazed at Caroline steadily. He was vastly pleased that she was to marry Bertram. Now that his sprite Ondine was fledged as a woman, he could have thought of no one more fitting to be her husband than Tom—Sir Thomas—for whom he had always retained a great admiration—a handsome, bold character such as James could never be. And how fortunate that she was a friend of his dear Susan; the rift between Sotherton and Mansfield Park would, after so many years, be truly mended at last.

Reverting to the practical, at a brief pause in the conversation James asked Tom, 'Where was it that the beast frightened the horses? It sounds as if there is a fence or wall gap somewhere.'

Tom considered. 'It was some way past the ruined mill; we had but just entered the wood leading to Long Hill.'

'Ah. That must have been on Bateson's

218

ground. What was the breed of the bullock?'

'A Hereford, I believe.'

'Yes; that would be Bateson's. I must let him know,' nodded James. 'It would be off his pasture on Long Hill. It was a Hereford?'

'Yes.'

'Well, that would be Bateson's, if it was a Hereford. I must tell him to look to his fences.'

James Rushworth's style of speech and thought was slow, but not unsound. He merely liked to be sure he had things quite right. Tom was for an instant tempted to reassure James that the bullock had been a Hereford, but he intercepted a glance that Susan cast towards her husband, of gentle affection with no hint of mockery; it seemed to Tom that, in a sense, Rushworth could depend on Susan—for a true estimation of his merits. Tom wished he had merits of his own for Caroline to encourage. Today might have punctured his conceit but it had roused a powerful desire for improvement that he was afraid he could not gratify, he could never make himself worthy of Caroline.

Today, there had been pleasure and excitement over the news of his engagement to Caroline but no mention of the future, of the when and way of the marriage; and Caroline, when Tom had ridden off and Susan took her up to see her to bed, felt some of the same anti-climax; she missed Tom already; without him she was worthless. She broke out:

'Oh, Susan, I could never be like you!'

'Like *me*? Why in the world should you?'

It was hard to explain. Caroline, impressed as she was by the splendour of Sotherton, had been as impressed by the way Susan fitted *in* here—Where she had only for a week or so been in residence—yet she knew the names of all the servants—addressed them with such casual command—presided so capably at the table—accepted such attributes as a personal maid—in fact, showed an authority and natural graciousness that one could only envy. Caroline tried to express this while Susan's brow knit in non-comprehension.

'I cannot feel that I . . . belong in Mansfield Park. You have seen the place where I was brought up—'

'My dear Caroline, I wish you could see the place where *I* was brought up. Dunsyke is palatial beside a tumbledown house in back-street Portsmouth. But I suppose,' Susan admitted with irony, 'the jealous might say that both you and I have done pretty well for ourselves.'

'Too well, in my case. To be "Lady" Bertram . . . And to be what Tom needs . . . To be to him what you are to James.'

She may have meant—and Susan understood—that James was an easier character altogether as a lifetime's companion, but Susan said with conviction:

'You *are* what Tom needs. He loves you. I should know,' she added, smiling, 'by the difference in him now, compared with his manner when he professed love for me. But, you must have a night's sleep, after such a day, and in the morning you will be happy again— happier than you have ever been in your life.'

Tom would have welcomed such encouragement. He slept ill, unable to quell his fears of being unworthy of Caroline, of her delicate sensibility and high principles. It seemed to him incredible that she should have accepted his proposal—she had been confused by her fall. He braced himself to tell his news to his mother, but not in the hope of much congratulations or reassurance.

Lady Bertram had retired before he reached home last night but this morning she had risen early and seemed unusually wide awake. As soon as he bade her good day she challenged him:

'What did Susan say in reply to my letter?'

'Your letter . . . ?' He tried to remember. 'Oh . . . I'm sorry, ma'am, but I forgot to give it to her—'

'That was thoughtless of you. I particularly wanted to ask whether at Sotherton they still rear those beautiful pheasants that I so much admired. I wanted to ask for a clutch of eggs to set for hatching before autumn. I wonder Caroline did not remind you of the letter—'

'Caroline . . .' echoed Tom as if still trying to remember. 'Caroline had a riding accident.' And as if in afterthought: 'Caroline and I are engaged to be married.'

With a disconcerting readiness Lady Bertram rejoined: 'Yes, I had supposed you would be, and I will tell you what I have been thinking: I am tired of that great cold master bedroom and I would like to move to the room in the west wing that has the morning sun. I will have new hangings and carpets and everything in pale blue. It will make a very pretty *boudoir* for me; perhaps I will sit up there in the mornings. But now, if you please, Tom, I would like my letter to be delivered, if you would send it over—'

'I will go myself,' said Tom with the utmost willingness. Eggs might be a slender pretext for another ten-mile ride, but he and the Sotherton party were well used to Lady Bertram's gentle imperiousness, and nor was he much surprised that eggs, blue *boudoirs* and her son's betrothal took that precedence in his mother's mind. So when he had discovered her letter still in the pocket of his riding coat, he sent for Harrier and set forth, at a speed impossible when travelling with a lady, and impeded by no stray livestock, to arrive at Sotherton unprepared and unexpected, which made his encounter with Caroline the more rapturous; as soon as their eyes met, they knew that there were no more doubts or hesitations. They fell in love all over again, and knew that it would last for ever.

Thus they supported one another when

their news was abroad and the practical plans formed. They would be married in October, after the harvest but before the approach of winter made travelling more difficult; the wedding of Sir Thomas Bertram, master of Mansfield Park, must be celebrated with due formality and feasting, and guests would be numerous.

'I shall have to have *more* new clothes!' declared Lady Bertram with no audible regret. At about this time she seemed to be emerging from her mourning, and not unwillingly; she developed a spirit of initiative that gave her new animation. At the wedding itself she was pleased to meet many friends among the neighbourhood whom she had neglected during her seclusion, and was as pleased that Tom invited them to dinner or card parties. At the wedding, too, she met again Mrs Rushworth who had—no one knew why—formed an attachment to Lady Bertram who soon after invited her to visit Mansfield Park; the two ladies chatted inconsequently and peacefully in the blue *boudoir*; before very long Mrs Rushworth, needing country air or threatened by worries in Bath, was to be found as often at Mansfield Park as at Sotherton.

Between Sotherton and Mansfield Park the bond necessarily remained close. When the bridegroom's brother was required to officiate at the second family wedding within a year, James Rushworth was called upon to give away

223

the bride; visiting between the houses was frequent and familiar; the Bertrams, should they wish to spend time in town, were welcome to borrow the house in Wimpole Street; but this was not often the case, since Sir Thomas was devoting his attention to his country duties. His niece Decima, bride's attendant, still hoped her Uncle Tom was not going to settle in his dull country-squire act, but she dared not say so; there was a new authority about him now that he was married, and, besides, it was likely that the Park would be less doleful under his reign than it had been of late.

Dull, Tom's life never was, for all its difficulties. There were always new projects to tempt him into new extravagances, even when he had given up his town house, gaming, theatricals and horse-racing. He had become aware of the plight of the aged, through his survey of his own dependants, and with the relatively negligible profit from the sale of the Antigua properties in his hand, he contrived to build and endow some almshouses down in the village, which he insisted on naming 'Caroline Cottages'. He studied new farming methods, put more land under the plough, and often submitted to the advice of the returned Stevenson if his innovations appeared over-ambitious. He asked Caroline:

'Does Mr Piper tell you how your friend Mr Trotter's tree-planting programme comes along? It sounds quite original.'

Mr Piper, too frail to travel to the wedding, was still an active source of news of Dunsyke, and had conveyed from Mr Trotter the hope that Sir Thomas and Lady Bertram would find it possible to visit Dunsyke—perhaps during the next summer, when the work of improving the estate should be well under way. Tom, for his part, was always eager to know more of Caroline, her life and background and family—every detail about these fascinated him—and so the visit was paid as soon as the Mansfield hay was in. Mr Trotter professed himself delighted by the condescension; to have his house haunted by titled persons, as well as by a poet, gave it a *cachet* he had not dared to expect. There was nothing fulsome about him as a host, though he had warned his womenfolk—newly arrived to live in the house—to remember their curtseys. His pampered but amusing daughters, horrified if truth be known by the rural bleakness of their surroundings, were grateful to Caroline for showing them the hidden beauties of her childhood's pleasures and hoped only that they need not stay over the winter but might flee back to the temperate climate of Manchester.

'Even so,' complained Miss Beatrix Trotter, as with her sister and Caroline she walked with Tom beside a sparkling beck, 'how are we to find husbands, in a place like this?'

Tom was fairly certain that very soon the

house would be in most elegant condition and that every eligible young man who could hold a gun would be paraded before these lucky (and no doubt well-dowered) young ladies; from a baronet, this prospect clearly gave the Miss Trotters fresh heart, delicately as Tom offered it.

Mr Brough meeting Caroline in the market square of Skenwith said gleefully: 'Was I not right? Dunsyke is going to raise the tone of the whole district! We shall soon have other old properties bought up and improved like this!'

Mr Piper on his garden bench among the murmuring bees said, sadly:

'I suppose it is bound to happen. We shall have the rich people as the cities spread, buying up the properties and tidying us up . . . I suppose it is progress?'

Tom and Caroline debated that issue during their homeward journey. It was evident to Caroline that Tom had considered all he had seen with serious attention; in company he had been 'Sir Thomas'; he had grown closer to her, sharing in her memories, seeing her as a more complete person; yet he had stood apart, himself complete in a new dignity; for the first time she saw him as . . . a baronet.

Others did. Even Culthorpe occasionally addressed him as 'Sir Thomas'. As his expertise advanced, he came to be considered by the countryside a model landlord, while the household at Mansfield Park was recognised as a model of domestic harmony, with its smooth and cheerful routine. On every fine morning, Maria Lady Bertram, dowager mother of Sir Thomas, could be seen setting out for the hatchery with pugs—and, later, grandchildren—trotting behind her to feed her pheasants.

We hope you have enjoyed this Large Print book. Other Chivers Press or Thorndike Press Large Print books are available at your library or directly from the publishers.

For more information about current and forthcoming titles, please call or write, without obligation, to:

Chivers Press Limited
Windsor Bridge Road
Bath BA2 3AX
England
Tel. (01225) 335336

OR

Thorndike Press
P.O. Box 159
Thorndike, Maine 04986
USA
Tel. (800) 223-2336

All our Large Print titles are designed for easy reading, and all our books are made to last.